QUEEN'S EDGE

THE HUNTER

BOOK FOUR

ELLE BEAUMONT

Midnight Tide
PUBLISHING

Content Warnings

This content contains depictions of graphic violence, profanity, gore, mention of sexual assault, and mention of abuse.

Contents

This one is for those who fix crooked crowns without ever saying a word.

ONE

Nothing had prepared me for the last few weeks of my life. Nothing. I was trained to be a queen— schooled in etiquette, politics, and diplomacy. Never had I been taught how to fight against an assassin. Never had I been taught how to win back my mate and the one I *loved*.

It was so foolish to love someone I hardly knew, yet here I was. And watching Niklaus be shot and dragged away was a memory that would be seared into my mind for a lifetime.

No matter how much I tried to scrub it from my mind, it always came back at night. If it hadn't been for Frederik, I would have run after the woman dragging Niklaus' body away. Yet the one who had begged and pleaded for me to stay ended up saving me.

Frederik was an odd boy, but he meant well. He explained how he knew Niklaus and owed him his life.

He also vowed that he'd help find him. He tried to soothe the silent tears that streamed down my cheeks too. But nothing eased the ache in my chest.

Much later, Captain Alric found us walking down the roadside. I was wearing Frederik's shirt, which was long enough to cover my essential pieces. He was horrified and ordered one of his men to offer their long coat at once.

I was mildly aware of Frederik snarling at their presence. I don't remember soothing all parties, but soon, we were on our way back to Mondwald Castle. Halfway there, we were stopped on the road and greeted by two individuals. They introduced themselves as the Huntsmen, Sabrina and Lukas Seidel, and said they were at my disposal.

That was two weeks ago, and I am as numb now as I was then.

My lessons never prepared me for this. Never.

MY FINGERS TWISTED around the fabric of my skirt, clenching and unclenching as I paced the war room in Abendrot castle. No matter how many times the Council said there was no outside threat, I didn't believe them. They were as blinded and foolish as my father, gods rest his soul.

Niklaus could be dead. No, I couldn't let myself think that way—I would have felt it.

I loathed most of the Council. They were rigid and treated me as if I were a toddler. The more I dealt with them, the more I realized they were likely the reason my father had turned to the Hawk.

"I cannot agree with you. If there was no threat, then my father would still hold the throne. In case you all are experiencing a momentary bout of forgetfulness, let me refresh your memory. King Ansgar is dead because he made a bargain with the wrong person, and she claimed his life." My pacing didn't cease until I reached the rectangular table and slammed my palms down on it.

Fear had lived in my heart these past weeks, but so had fury, and with the two side by side, I had little to no patience for their idiocy.

One man looked up at me, eyes wide and mouth open in shock. "I beg your pardon?"

"Beg if you'd like, but I won't pardon willful ignorance. I am not my father. I won't tolerate blatant ignorance. Do you think you'd be sitting where you are now if the Hawk swept through the entire kingdom's hierarchical system?" I lifted my palms from the table and clasped my hands in front of me, not waiting for an answer. "I doubt it." I paused for a minute and walked toward a window on the far side of the room. I glanced outside Abendrot's castle, missing the more simplistic view from Mondwald. "I appreciate you all for coming, but I invited you here to discuss immediate changes in the kingdom."

"What changes?" councilwoman, Lady Hines asked.

I turned from the window, addressing the table with a hard stare. "Effective immediately, Bromiel will begin logging and open for trade. Walddorf will begin exporting goods, and so will our angry brethren in Brigmoor. It's time we unite our country and strengthen our alliances."

"What!?" the Council shouted collectively.

"You can't!"

"Outrageous. The king never . . ."

I pressed my lips together and nodded my head. "The king never did much for our citizens. I loved my father dearly, but he had his faults, and one of them was crippling our villages and cities. We have much to offer, and by choking off our resources, we suffocate ourselves. If my father had opened more trade, we wouldn't have had to look for funds from elsewhere. I will reach out to the few alliances we still have and attempt to strengthen our bonds with them."

"It isn't such a preposterous idea," Lord Aksel chimed in, stroking his bearded chin. "We could do with strengthening the alliances. And the previous talks of strengthening our villages again by exporting goods, I think this would serve us all well." His agreement stirred the pot. Reminding them of the dangers during such an uncertain time.

A collective argument burst from the table. I was the topic, but I didn't join in the argument. If I'd let them, they likely would have torn each other's clothes to pieces.

"Enough! Gather your wits. We have a lot to discuss here today." I surveyed the angry faces, but in the depths of their eyes was fear, and I knew that sentiment too well. Fear whispered to me at night, taunting me with failures that hadn't occurred yet and worst-case scenarios, but I was still in control here.

"Such as your coronation," the one woman sneered.

"And the chatter of war!" A hand slammed against the table as the councilman shouted.

Heat filled my cheeks. It crept into my ears and stung my eyes, but I wouldn't falter in front of these people. "Collect yourselves," I hissed, pinching the bridge of my nose to ground myself. "I have decided to postpone the coronation. It isn't safe, which I think you can all agree on. If there is no war, then we can hold the coronation in the spring." Most nodded their heads in agreement.

"Who is chattering about war?" the bishop inquired.

"Who isn't? And where have you been hiding? Tucked away with your books, are you?" the woman snapped.

The bishop's face reddened, his nostrils flaring. "Better that than with numerous men."

If I had to douse them in water, I would. I eyed the pitcher and contemplated it, but I wanted them to take me seriously, not to see me as a hot-tempered child. "Enough of your bantering. Everyone is chattering about it. We are seen as weak right now, and maybe we are, but this is why I aim to reach out to our alliances. I suggest all of you rally our country-folk. We *all* need unity. Is that understood?"

"Yes, Your Highness," they muttered collectively.

I swept a strand of white hair from my face and flicked my hand. "That is all. It's not up for debate. Good day, Council." Before I lost my nerve, I turned on my heels and left the room.

My heart pounded violently in my chest, and once outside the war room, I cupped a hand over my mouth. I didn't realize Captain Alric was standing against the wall, not until he spoke.

"Are you all right, Your Highness?" He pushed off the wall and closed the space between us.

I exhaled and motioned for him to follow me. I didn't want to hear what the Council had to say about me, and I didn't want them to see my composure crumble. "I will be. I don't think they were expecting to hear that." My gaze flicked toward Alric, and I knew he had heard my shouting. Neither the walls nor door would have concealed it.

Alric smiled wryly. "Maybe not, but it's what they needed to see and hear. Now they understand they aren't dealing with a little lamb. You are a *wolf*. I think it's time to let everyone know that."

His words caught me by surprise, but I didn't falter in my stride. I wondered what he meant for a moment, but then I realized Alric was right. Niklaus had been right too. The kingdom needed me for who I was, not who I longed to be or pretended to be. Abendrot needed a wolf—a strong leader who wouldn't back down.

"Thank you. I think you're right."

He chuckled. "This is one of the few things I know

I'm right about." He paused before continuing, "I also think you'd benefit from some combat training. It would help ease some of your tension, and when I'm not free, I know Raif can assist you."

I considered his words and nodded. "I agree. I wouldn't mind that at all."

Alric bowed his head. "Will you be needing me anymore?"

"No, thank you."

After I dismissed Alric, I headed down to the garden. I assumed Elka would be there, as had been her habit almost every day for a week. When she thought no one was looking, she'd meet with Raif and it made me smile to think of how far she'd come. Elka had always feared werewolves, and when the full moon would rise, she had seemed extra fidgety around me. Now, it was lessening.

Change is happening before your eyes.

Once outside, the sun shone brightly and offered little warmth. Winter was in full swing, and she wouldn't be letting up anytime soon. Snow would soon powder the ground, which brought forth memories of playing with Edda in the fresh snow. A sob choked me as I wound through the garden. I refused to cry. I hadn't let tears fall for two weeks, and I wouldn't start now.

"My lady!" Elka called and stood from the bench she was perched on. "Do you need me? We are almost finished here." She motioned to Raif and smiled.

It wasn't lost on me how much time Elka spent with Rolph—or rather, Raif, as I had come to learn was his true name. She was one of the few in the castle who could communicate with him properly, but I saw the way she smiled and the way his eyes lit up every time she approached. I was happy for my maid and jealous that she had him within reach. Jealous because I wished Niklaus was here instead. It was a wicked thought to have.

Kina had healed but had been left with terrible scarring on her arm. She returned to the Huntsmen since Edda wasn't . . . since Kina was of more use with them.

"No, I knew you'd be here. I wanted to check in and see how Raif was faring. You look well. A lot better than you did last week."

Raif signed a "thank you" and then a series of other hand gestures I couldn't understand. Luckily, Elka did and translated them.

"He says he feels better." Elka shared a look with him, and he signed to her. "He wants to know if you're all right, my lady."

In truth, I wasn't all right. I was alive, but the gnawing feeling of being separated from Niklaus was maddening. "I will be." It was all I managed to say.

Raif stood from the bench and walked toward me. He pointed, moving both his hands toward his shoulders before pushing them outward with clenched fists. I didn't know what he was saying, but he repeated it again, and then again. Each time he brought his clenched fists out, it was as if he was showing off his muscles—or strength. I put two and two together.

"I don't feel strong," I replied.

Raif pointed at me and nodded before he gingerly

wrapped his arms around me. My body sighed against his, welcoming the warmth and wishing it was someone else.

"I will find Niklaus, and then I will kill *her*. The Hawk will pay for everything she has done." My voice sounded cold even to my ears, but Raif didn't pull away, he just nodded his head in agreement.

Later on, when the Council had left and the unwelcome quiet settled over the castle, I hid away in the study. The sound of shuffling feet, hushed conversations, and the occasional order from a guard took the place of Edda's laughter. I loathed the fact that there was little I could do but be ready, and this was how I would prepare.

I pulled out pieces of paper and a quill to write. Everything was about to change in Abendrot, and I hoped it was for the best. It was time to address Bromiel's forestry, Walddorf's meat and fur, and even our chilly brethren in Brigmoor with their fresh fish and shipbuilding. Perhaps I could mend the wounds my father had torn open during his reign.

When my wrist ached, my head throbbed, and my eyes could no longer focus on the wobbling words before me, I put the quill back and sealed the letters. I would send them to the village head, and tomorrow, I'd begin penning my letters to our neighboring alliances outside of the country.

I didn't know if they wanted to hear from Abendrot, much less me, but I didn't have a choice. I was now the ruler of the kingdom.

Two

NIKLAUS

A beautiful female turned her back to me, inching her chemise down until it slipped down her curves and pooled at her bare feet. Her ivory hair hung in a messy braid, nearly tickling the small of her back. I'd only seen the shade on someone as young as her once before, and that was—

She spun around to face me.

Princess Stasya.

She closed the distance between us, her fingers coaxing my shirt up.

Why the hell was I dreaming about the princess like this? Even as my thoughts raced, I shifted forward, yearning to feel her skin quiver beneath my touch.

"Niklaus," she sighed my name, further stirring desire.

How did she know my name, my true name?

The creaking of floorboards roused me. I sat up,

blinking away the sleep, and winced from the pounding behind my eyes. Lethe had that effect on people. My mother used to sit me down at the table, talk about the tinctures and herbs she could use to help others. Even the ones that seemed only harmful.

Even Lethe had a purpose in life: to help ease painful pasts. She told me once that werewolves needed higher doses of the drug because our bodies fought stronger than a human's.

It wasn't until this week that the dreams had started to trickle in. Only, a deep part of me knew it wasn't just that.

"I hope it was a good memory," Ashroy muttered.

"Memory?"

Ashroy inched closer to the bars separating us. "Your memories will return, but I can't say when. When they begin to, you'll dream of what has been forgotten." His pale brows lifted, and he tilted his head. His high cheek bones were even more pronounced now from weight loss.

Normally, I wouldn't care if I told him exactly what the dream was about, but this one felt private. I lifted my hand to my neck, where Ashroy claimed I'd had a mark. Was it from her?

Why would I ever mate with the princess? King Ansgar was nothing but a filthy swine. And one of his daughters was in the cell next to me, while the other was plaguing me in my sleep.

"I know you think I'm mad for suggesting that you're an elite assassin—"

"Not really," I chuckled. "Death is my forte." All those years in the butcher shop? While it wasn't a human's life, I had no doubt I could cut down a deserving victim, no payment required. A poacher? I'd not think twice about it. Still, I didn't know why I should trust someone I didn't know.

"Tell me what you dreamed of this time," Ashroy sighed, leaning his head against the bars of his cell. For as smart-mouthed as he could be, he seemed to have infinite patience. Not that there was much else to do down here but endure one another's company.

When I told him about the last dream I had, Ashroy referred to a group of assassins called the Huntsmen, whom I was apparently affiliated with. *Assassin.* Shifting my jaw, I glanced over at him and then down at Edda, who was sleeping against him.

"You don't want to know," I offered. "She was undressing—"

"You're right. I don't want to know." He grimaced and glanced at my neck again. "But that explains the mark you had when you arrived. It confirms my suspicion of you mating with Stasya."

Princess Stasya was . . . my mate? A pulse inside of my chest said this was right, that she was. However, there was no memory supporting this save for the vague dream.

"As long as there are those memories, there is hope," Ashroy said, lowering his voice as Edda stirred. "And remember, Niklaus: Whatever you do, if Domitia offers you freedom, don't return home. If you return home, she'll kill your family."

Largely, I didn't want to trust him. But the way he spoke, the way his eyes implored me, I felt inclined to believe him. He was a witch, that I could sniff out, even with his collar on, and I didn't know him. Domitia could have planted him here to confuse me further or test me. Still, when he was warning me to not visit my family, I vowed not to.

Moments later, the door at the stairwell opened, and footsteps carried down. When the shadowed figure stepped into view, I didn't have to see her face to know that it was Domitia. Since waking two weeks ago, I'd noticed she had used perfume—gardenia, if I wasn't mistaken. Maybe it was because she didn't need to sneak into places anymore. It was easy to scent her arrival now.

"Incoming," I muttered to my cellmates.

"Bite your tongue and try to get out so you can learn something." Ashroy leaned his head toward Edda, feigning sleep as our guest of honor arrived.

"Well, dear hunter, are you ready to play nice?" She stepped closer, but not close enough that I could reach through the bars and ensnare her.

"I think you have a different definition of 'playing nice,'" I said from where I sat in the corner of my prison.

Domitia's gaze flicked between me and the cell next to me before forcing a smile. "My, it seems we both have a sense of humor today." She stepped closer, still out of my reach, and leaned forward. If I jammed my arm through the rungs, I could almost grab her unbound hair.

And then what?

"Are you willing to be civil today? I was thinking we could discuss matters upstairs. Over a roast."

I hadn't eaten a decent meal in two weeks, and my traitorous stomach growled. "Yes." In truth, I had lashed out every time she approached. Every time she dangled a bloody opportunity in front of me. But even amid my confusion, I refused to let her know how much I remembered, considering I wasn't supposed to remember a damn thing. But I did . . . I recalled my family, the butcher shop, and my wretched sire. The timelines were fuzzy. In my mind, Liesel was only thirteen, but how old was she truly? How old was I?

And why did she need to give me lethe to begin with?

Domitia was clever, which was why she stood in front of a cell, and I had to be as clever or more so. I had to play along with her games.

"If you promise a steak and eggs, I'll consider behaving for you." My gaze shifted over her shoulder, where guards stepped forward.

"I can see about that." She motioned toward her lackeys, and one stepped forward, unlocking the door.

Said man slid a pair of manacles from his hip and grunted. "Hands behind your back and stand up."

With a sigh, I stood and held my hands behind my back. I had to show that I was compliant, and then maybe Domitia would talk. Explain herself . . .

The guard shoved me out of the cell, and I stumbled

forward, catching myself before I collided with Domitia. She was tall for a woman but still only came up to my shoulder.

She dragged her fingertip along my cheek, which had grown a thicker coating of hair given that I hadn't had the chance to shave. "I like this. It gives you a feral appearance."

I couldn't imagine what I looked like. Unruly hair, filthy, and with a thick layer of scruff. I'm sure I looked feral.

"Lead the way, my lady," I said, trying to keep my tone level and without a bite. I needed to play along with her game until I knew my surroundings better.

Domitia turned her back to me, and her guards followed to my left and right. With my wits more about me than last time, I counted the steps, took note that we were not in a dungeon but a wine cellar. Shelf upon shelf was lined with bottles, and there were even a few wooden barrels shoved into a corner.

The only visible exit was the stairwell.

Domitia ascended the stairs and brought me down a hallway, toward a finely furnished dining room that was vaguely familiar. A dark oak table sat in the middle of the room surrounded by high-backed chairs with deep blue cushions. No pictures decorated the white walls, but a singular golden figurine of a hawk sat on the mantle above the fireplace.

"Sit," she ordered.

Everything in me wanted to lash out, to rebel against her order, but if I wanted any chance of gaining the upper hand, I had to earn her trust. In the end, I complied and lowered myself into a chair.

Domitia sat at the opposite end of the table and flicked her fingers at a guard. "Tell the cook to prepare steak and eggs for our guest." She smiled and leaned her chin into her palm. "Now, I'll let you in on a little secret because I think we're coming to understand one another." There was a rather sensuous quality to her. Perhaps it was her curves that were hardly concealed by the form-fitting dress she wore. The deep V-neck of her dress put her breasts on display, and the high slit of her skirt allowed an ample view of what she had to offer. Or maybe it was her full lips that one knew would feel sinfully good as they coasted over their skin. It was likely all of that.

Except, she was a devil.

"I'm listening," I said, inclining my head as I balanced on the edge of my chair. It wasn't exactly comfortable to sit with my hands cuffed behind my back.

"You see, Abendrot is owed to me through a bargain, and I'm here to claim it. And I want you to help me in two ways. Break Princess Stasya." She said this, seeming to watch for an indication that I had any form of attachment toward her. I willed my heart to keep its steady pace. "And rip the Council to pieces. Now that Ansgar is gone, the eradication of werewolves is off the table."

Six nobles sat on the Council, six that either Ansgar had selected or his father before him had. None of them were good people, in my opinion. Otherwise, they would have fought harder to knock sense into Ansgar.

Although, that was unfair, Lord Aksel never did agree with the king's politics, and everyone was aware of that.

I kept having to remind myself that the king was dead, that it was Domitia who had killed him, per Ashroy. And she was only confirming what he said.

"So, you need me to kill people for you?" The scent of steak wafted toward me, and I turned in the direction it came from. My mouth watered as the cook brought a sirloin cut toward me, covered in butter and eggs. Was she only going to tease me with food or actually let me eat? This was probably a test. "I have no love for the Council. They've failed the kingdom and deserve punishment."

Domitia motioned toward her guard, and he leaned forward to unlock my manacles. "Good. Then you may eat, because you're going to need your strength for what comes next."

THREE

Sleep evaded me again. I woke in the middle of the night with the phantom feeling that Niklaus was next to me. When my eyes opened and I saw nothing but a pillow, I hurled it across the room and opted to write letters to our alliances.

By the time I finished, the sun peeked through my window and bathed my desk in light. Today would be another busy day. My decisions would have repercussions, and I had to remember what Alric told me. *You are a wolf. It is time to let everyone know that.*

And I would. It wasn't a curse, and it wasn't a weakness. Not like my father had told me time and time again. It was a strength—one that I would embrace. If I had to howl from every balcony, I would, and I'd let the kingdom know that the time for hunting werewolves, the time for turning a blind eye, was through.

I heard their pleas. I saw their sorrows. And I would

change *everything*. I couldn't fix *my* sorrow, and I couldn't stop from pleading with whatever gods listened to me at night, but I could help my people.

A knock on the door broke my internal speech. Half dozing at the desk, it took a moment to grab my robe and wrap it around myself. When I answered the door, Elka's brown eyes stared up at me.

"I know it's early, my lady, but you have visitors." She worried on her lower lip, like she always did when she was nervous.

"It *is* early. Tell them to go away. Why were they even let inside at this hour?" I scrubbed my face with a hand, trying to rub what I'm sure was annoyance off of it.

Elka shifted, turning to look down the hall. "It's the huntsmen. They insisted on entering, and Captain Alric allowed it. He thought they may have information—it seems they do." She paused for a moment and then, "Would you like for me to dress you?"

I flung open the door as "Huntsmen" registered. "Yes. You could have told me it was them when I answered." As soon as Elka shut the door, I shed my nightgown and walked toward where my dress hung.

"I'm sorry, my lady. I'll be as quick as possible."

And she was. Elka was a flurry of movement as she pulled the stays and tied them up. She was quick with my hair too, which she re-braided and coiled at the back of my head.

"All done!" she chirped and opened the door for me.

I wore a deep purple floor-length dress with an opalescent silk sheer wrapping around my body and trailing behind me. It would have been cold for a human, but I wasn't even chilled.

All but running down the hall and the stairs, I approached the grand entrance and found Lukas and Sabrina Seidel speaking to Alric. Behind the twins, Frederik shuffled from foot to foot.

"Have any of you eaten yet?" I inquired.

"No. I'm hungry!" Frederik blurted and ducked his head when all eyes fell on him.

"Very well, let's have breakfast." I turned and led them toward the dining hall.

The smell of sweetmeat pies wafted through the halls, alerting my stomach that it had been awake for quite some time and hadn't eaten yet. I saw a servant poke their head into the dining hall as we arrived, then she scooted back into the cubby she'd come from.

"Is there news?" I asked abruptly. Motioning to the chairs around the table, I took a seat at the head and waited for someone—anyone—to answer.

The twins shared a brief look, and then Sabrina spoke. "We believe we found the manor where your sister, Niklaus, and Prince Ashroy are being held captive." There was an unspoken "if everyone is still alive" that hung between us. "We have been moving as quickly as we can without raising suspicions."

Those were not the words I wanted to hear. I wanted to hear that we were charging forward with a plan to extract them—but no, it was more waiting, more time for things to go awry. With every passing moment, dread's teeth sank deeper and deeper into my heart.

I leaned back as the kitchen maid served us, keeping tight-lipped on what I wanted to say in front of them. When they left, I leaned forward and spoke through gritted teeth. "So, all we have is a *maybe* on their whereabouts. I don't call that news."

Frederik's fingers clutched onto his utensil, the muscles in his face tightening as he looked from me to the twins. I had to calm down, if not for my sake, then Fred's. The Seidels had told me more than once since taking him in that he needed a stable environment, that they'd witnessed him breaking down, and it wasn't safe.

Sabrina kept her expression schooled, showing no sign that my words irked her. "With all due respect, Your Highness, we are not *spies*. What has your team dredged up?" She lifted her fork and took a bite of the pie as she watched me.

She was right. "My apologies. I realize you're doing all you can. I said it before, but I mean it, my people can help you. If a spy is what you need, we'll find one—or however many are required. I just want all of them back." My bottom lip quivered from a mixture of frustration and despair.

It was Lukas who spoke up next. "We'll take whoever you offer to us. We want Niklaus back too. It isn't easy lying to his family about where he has been."

I hadn't thought of them, not even a little. I was so wrapped up in my grief that I hadn't even stopped to consider how his family must have felt. "I selfishly forgot all about them."

"Well, you've been preoccupied, Your Highness."

Sabrina picked away at her plate. "Before this started, he had told his family he was involved with protecting you. And when he returns, it'll be up to him to reach out to them."

When, I thought, *when he returns*. I preferred that to *if*.

Frederik stood, his palms down on the table as he looked at me with his pale green eyes. "He will return. I will help like I promised. He'll come back, you'll see, and—"

Lukas shifted, but he wasn't the one to speak. It was Sabrina. "Nik will come back, Fred. But we talked about you helping, remember? You can stay here and protect the princess."

"No," said Frederik. Clarity came to his eyes as he stared at me. "I promised I'd help, and I will. So train me, help me, or don't. I'll do it myself if I have to." He spoke so plainly that in that moment, he reminded me of Niklaus. As if he was ready to take on the entire world, knowing death awaited him.

Before an argument broke out—or worse—I lifted my hand and quieted all of them. "Perhaps it wouldn't be such a terrible idea. If Frederik wishes to be trained, either one of my men or yours can help him." My gaze switched from Lukas to Sabrina as I spoke. "Otherwise, anything short of chaining him up won't stop him. I know that look well. I also don't suggest tying him down."

Frederik sat down, bowing his head as he quieted. "Please don't chain me. I don't like it. *He* used to do that to me," he muttered beneath his breath. And just like that, the clarity drifted away.

"No one will do that, Frederik. No one." I lifted my fork and let the conversation die there. "They say a blizzard is due to hit us soon." I looked up at Lukas. His lips pressed into a firm line as he nodded.

"That's usually when beasts hunker down in their dens. It makes it easier to hunt them when you're waiting outside their shelter."

I savored a piece of the sweet meat as I listened to him. "Is that so?" I paused, and then, "Clever tactic." I gave him a subtle nod. If Lukas had been looking for permission without asking verbally, he had it. "Well, eat up. It's fresh, and I'd hate for it to grow cold."

The rest of breakfast was relatively quiet, except for a few small conversations, which seemed to relax Frederik. By the time we finished eating, my day of answering missives and entertaining disgruntled citizens was calling me—or at least what I thought would be disgruntled individuals.

The throne room had always been one of my favorites when I was little. Not because of what it represented but because it was lit by a massive, domed window behind the throne. Sitting wolves perched on the two banisters that framed the stairs to the throne. Despite my father's contempt for werewolves, he'd kept them on our banners and hidden in plain sight. He'd told me it was because of the strength they represented. The fear they instilled.

The cream walls were shades lighter than the rest of

the rooms in the castle. Dark wood contrasted with the lightness from the walls, but when I was young, it wasn't the glass that caught my attention, nor the way my father looked on the throne. No, it was the ornate ceiling. Hand-carved wooden embellishments decorated the walls, but the ceiling was a mixture of paints—gold, cream, sea green.

Sometimes, I wondered what had happened to the portraits that belonged to the rightful royal family. If they were stored somewhere, or if they'd been burned when the humans took over.

My thoughts were interrupted when the steward announced the first person. To my surprise, the visitor smiled from ear to ear as he bowed. In his hands, he wrung his hat nervously but didn't exude hatred or discontent.

"Your Highness, first of all, I am grateful to you. It's only that, we in Bromiel, we wish to ask for help in logging, as we have such a large volume and are new to the idea. Bromiel is still poor and . . . we ask for aid, so we can grow, Your Highness." He bowed his head, rocking from foot to foot.

It was too soon for them to have received my missive, and so he didn't know yet of my plans. "Rest assured, your village head will receive a letter soon proposing just that. It's time that Bromiel and the rest of Abendrot is taken care of."

"Thank you, thank you so much, Your Highness."

Next, a woman stepped forward. She wore a ragged cloak, and her shoes looked worn through. When I really looked her over, I didn't think she was much older than me, but there were dark circles beneath her eyes, an exhaustion that aged her deeply.

"Your Highness, I've come to thank you, and, if you'll accept it . . . a token of gratitude for the shipments of medicine. You see—" She sucked in a breath. "My daughter was among the ill, and without the help she so desperately needed, she would have been among the other fallen."

I hadn't forgotten the sickness spreading through the kingdom, but with everything else going on, it hadn't been at the forefront of my mind. This was something I had pushed for prior to my father's death. It gladdened my heart to hear a spot of good news, to receive praise instead of being told what had been done wrong or what I was doing wrong.

Alric stood by my side, so the moment the woman stepped forward, he did too, barring her path. "No farther."

"She's fine." I motioned for her to step forward. "What is your name?"

"Katherine," she supplied and bowed her head. "It's not much, but it is a small token of thanks." She reached into the satchel on her person, and Alric tensed. However, since she had been allowed inside this far, I didn't worry. Her bag had been searched prior to entering. Katherine pulled out a dark green knitted piece and closed the distance between us. "It's a capelet. The softest wool grown from our sheep. I dyed it and knitted it. Please accept this."

Such a simple thing, but it touched me beyond words. I took the piece and held it up, marveling at the effort that had gone into making it. "That is so kind of you." I hugged it to my chest. "I am glad your little girl is well again.

One by one, they all came, until it was well past noon and my head throbbed. I saw them all, though. Everyone that had waited to see me.

The lack of sleep finally caught up to me, and instead of taking a midday meal, I opted for a retreat to my room. I didn't intend to slumber, all I wanted was quiet, but as I lay down on the bed, sleep pulled me under. This time, when I dreamed, I didn't fall into a nightmare.

I saw Niklaus.

He stood in front of me, dressed in black breeches, knee-high boots, and a white shirt that had come untucked. The stays at his throat had come undone and loosened, exposing the pale skin beneath and the smattering of freckles there.

"Why do I have to learn this dance?" His crooked grin faltered, and his hands squeezed my hips, and I no longer wished to dance with him but to take him to my quarters.

"Because every royal s—" I stopped myself, but I should have known better than to begin something I didn't intend to finish, especially in Niklaus' company.

His fingers caught my chin, and he leaned in. "A what?"

Every inch of me warmed. A tingling sensation rippled through me, and I knew it was desire. "Royal spy." He leaned in closer as I spoke, teasing my lips so carelessly.

"That was weak." Niklaus caught my lips between his and

tugged me against his chest. "Finish what you were going to say. Or I'll force it out."

I delighted in those words, shivering in anticipation of how he wanted to draw them out of me. "What are you going to do —" I gasped as he bit my neck, sending a mixture of excitement and pain through me. "Spouse! Royal spouse."

Niklaus' eyes widened as he pulled back. "You're proposing to me?" He didn't mock me, but he also didn't let me duck my head into his chest to hide. Both of his hands slid up to cup my cheeks, and he held my gaze.

"I thought, since we—we are mates now." Words jumbled around in my head as I tried to clarify what I meant. "If you wanted someone else, then forget it." The words came out a little sharper than I intended, but Niklaus didn't flinch.

"No. I merely wished for you to say it."

"I hate you," I whispered.

Niklaus' lips skimmed mine, teasing me, making me crave more than the featherlight touch. "No, you don't."

The dream faded into blackness. It was sweet and realistic, which brought tears to my eyes. A hole had been torn open inside my chest, and with each passing day, it tore even wider. My sister was gone, and so was my mate. The Hawk would pay for taking them from me. I would kill her.

Four

Another week had passed, and my patience was wearing thin. Three weeks since they abducted my sister and Prince Ashroy. Nearly a whole bloody month since that nightmarish display of Niklaus being dragged off. I needed to know he was alive.

The gods must have been tired of me praying or cursing them because I had an answer soon enough.

The carriage halted, and when I glanced out the window, I spied the castle's courtyard and Captain Alric as he approached the door. He barely had the time to open it before the steward raced forward, a missive in his hand.

"Your Highness!" Steward Thomas rushed. "It's the bishop." He panted, pausing as he drew in a breath.

I'd been in Bromiel all morning, ensuring that supplies had arrived for the village to begin their new industry. Judging by the sun, it was likely mid-afternoon. Life could change at the drop of a hat, but gods above, I was tiring of that!

"What about the bishop, Thomas?" I slid from the carriage, eyeing Thomas as he stammered and paled considerably. "How?"

"Foul play, they say. Killed in his sleep."

"Did you hear anything else?" I asked slowly. Goose-bumps dotted my skin as I wondered if this had been Niklaus, or if this was the Hawk playing a game. I needed to know or see some kind of sign that he was alive.

"There was a note left." The steward blanched. "It read: 'One pig for the slaughter.'"

"Where is it?" I approached him, focusing on the steward's expression. He wobbled where he stood, likely from the adrenaline. I should have felt the same, but a part of me knew where those words had come from. "The note. Was it brought here?" I plucked at the gloves covering my fingers and stormed past the dumbstruck man.

"Alric, find out where that note is and bring it to me immediately." I knew Nik's chicken scratch, and while I didn't doubt the Hawk could easily have him scribble down a foolish line, it would still be his penmanship.

My heart skipped when they brought the note to me at supper. They couldn't smell it, but I could. Soft pine and earthy musk clung to the paper, making it painfully obvious to me that Niklaus had touched it, and it was a fresh scent.

"It's the Big Bad Wolf." I used his moniker. He had

two sides to him, and while I knew both, I loved Niklaus von Brandt. Aloof, playful, and quick-witted, that was the male I knew. I wiped my mouth, tossed the cloth onto the table, and sprang from my chair. "Send for the Huntsmen. We need to talk."

I COULDN'T REFRAIN from pacing. The Seidels arrived just before I wore a hole in the study's rug. Raif had done his best to calm me, and his sister Kina was attempting to distract me with food, and when that failed, it was letters from officials.

"It's Niklaus, I can smell it. I also know that's his handwriting," I said as soon as the twins entered the room. I lifted the paper in my hand, waving it like a flag. "My sister is rotting in a cell or worse, so if you sit on your hands once more, I will decline your aid and move forward without you."

Sabrina's brows lifted, and her eyes narrowed a moment later, but it was her twin who spoke. "We haven't been idle. With the aid of your spies and our team, we've been able to infiltrate the manor the Hawk lives in. Her real name is Lady Domitia, and knowing that . . ." Lukas paused and pulled a piece of paper from his coat. "She is wicked, with a lot of power behind her. Which is fine because we enjoy a challenge."

I snatched the paper from Lukas and stared down at

it. The note detailed who Lady Domitia was and what she had done in the last several years. My blood chilled as I read through her accomplishments. She could bring a country down and had done so to a smaller country than Abendrot. The mere idea formed a pit in my stomach, and I didn't know how we'd survive this—how Abendrot would survive.

"We must stop her," I hissed.

"We have a plan," the twins said in unison, leaving Raif, Kina, and me to listen.

By the end of the discussion, we had a plan to move forward as early as the end of the week, which delighted me. Finally, we'd have this bird where she belonged: buried in the ground.

Lukas cocked his head, squinting at Raif. "Are you sure you're up for this? It hasn't been that long since the attack."

Raif nodded.

"All right, fair enough. It's a plan, then."

After that meeting, we all left feeling as though we had accomplished something. We even assigned more guards to those on the Council and inside the castle.

When morning came, a servant delivered another slip of paper to me. I glanced down, reading the words: "Two piggies more for thee." Blood stained the bottom of the parchment, and the way the ink was smeared, I could tell Niklaus had been in a rush.

I crumpled the paper in frustration. "I'd ask how this keeps happening, but I know how." Wrenching my eyes shut, I forced the threat of tears away and focused on the fury, let it fuel me.

"This is what she does. Domitia is from Muzsreshka, and we know what happened to the last king."

They never found the culprits who'd assassinated him, but soon, a new, younger king sat on the throne. Muzsreshka's growing power and territorial claims forced new alliances to form and old ones to crumble.

"She breaks the kingdoms down from the inside out. Builds a new structure in whatever way she and her cohorts see fit." He dragged a hand down his face. "She typically starts from the bottom and works her way up. I'm not certain why she started with your father first." He chewed his bottom lip, and then continued. "She also had a hand in Kunai." A small tropical kingdom, but beautiful as far as I'd heard. "She helped frame the queen, had her beheaded, and a new queen now sits on the throne. They use the term 'kingmaker.'" Lukas paused and tilted his head. "But she will see to putting a new king or queen on the throne if the price is right."

Tension rippled through me. "Are we still waiting until the end of this week to infiltrate the manor Raif located?"

The twins shared a look and then turned to me, nodding. "Yes. We're still waiting for your alliances to answer your letters so that they're in place for us too."

So we waited, and each day, a new member of the Council died. Until there was only one—Lord Aksel.

Niklaus had completed the sordid rhyme.

One little pig for the slaughter,
Two piggies more for thee.
Three little pigs full of greed
And four more dead, you see.
Five little pigs who deserved it, and five more it'll be.
Until I cleanse the kingdom of filth.
This is the Wolf's decree.

I didn't mourn the loss of all but one of the Council in the way I should have, but fear tangled my wits. Their absence was noted throughout the kingdom though, as more and more tasks fell onto me and Lord Aksel, and also onto less qualified individuals. I found it increasingly difficult to rationalize all of this madness and to keep my country calm while I felt as though I was descending into a pit of despair. How was I to protect them when I couldn't protect those closest to me?

I was next on that list. And this time, I didn't have Niklaus on my side to protect me. If I'd thought the security had increased before, it was tenfold now. A guard stood at my window, and two were on either side of the door just outside my room. Privacy had become a thing of the past, all for the sake of protecting me.

At the end of the week, Raif approached me, tapped my arm, and signed, "Today, we go." His fingers moved slowly for my benefit.

Today. As I sighed in relief, my shoulders sagged. When I moved to the window and glanced outside, I saw that a thick blanket of snow coated the land. Snow that must have been knee-deep. "In this snow?"

Raif nodded. "The Hawk left. We will get Princess Edda and Prince Ashroy."

Hope blossomed in my chest, although I didn't dare to do more than that. I'd get my sister back, and Ashroy . . . "Niklaus?"

"The last we knew, he was still there. But our source didn't say."

Niklaus would have to wait, I knew that. Getting my sister back was more important than anything. Niklaus would survive, but who could say the same for my sister and the prince? Reports had said they were alive and well considering the circumstances, but what did that mean? They were prisoners, and the Hawk had yet to show an ounce of mercy.

I must have been clutching the drape in my grasp because Raif gently took my hand in his and wrapped me in a hug. His warmth comforted me; the scents of smoke, metal, and a woodsy musk that was wholly Raif invaded my senses.

When he released me, he pointed at me and signed, "Wolf." His lips tilted up into a kind smile, but he emphasized the word again and nodded.

I was a wolf, and everyone kept reminding me of that, but it was time I truly embraced it. The country needed a wolf now more than ever.

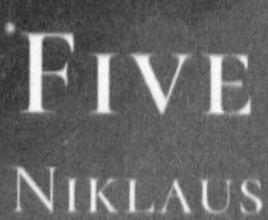

FIVE

NIKLAUS

Domitia left not long ago to meet with her arriving forces, and for some reason, she didn't throw me back in my cell like she usually did. She allowed me this freedom. Perhaps it was another one of her games, but I wasn't going to waste too much time dwelling on why.

I had proven to myself that I could handle the heavily guarded house, even if it was an obstacle. Each of the Council I'd cut down had guards too. And they were currently six feet under. Save for one—Lord Aksel, and his time was short.

While I had been out last, I'd made certain to pass missives along from Ashroy to Ishkertov, which was easy enough since all I needed was to find a messenger.

Standing from the dining table, I scooped up the basket of rolls and strolled toward the kitchen. The cook yelped as he spun around and faced me.

"Can you make two other plates?" I grabbed a roll and popped the whole thing in my mouth, chewing it quickly.

"S-sure." The cook was a portly man, with salt-and-pepper hair that hung limply at his shoulders. He made quick work of preparing the bacon, eggs, and sausage links before whirling around with the plates in his grasp. "Where to?"

"I've got them." I took the plates from him, balancing them on a forearm. "Forks?" The cook slid them onto the plate, and I left the kitchen, wound my way down a hall, and stopped at the door leading to the basement.

A guard glanced at me and lifted a brow. "Breakfast?"

I didn't recognize this guard. Domitia had brought in new recruits prior to leaving, and this man looked to be in his mid-thirties. A finely groomed dark beard covered his face, and his dark hazel eyes followed my movements, but he lacked the bite the other guards seemed to have with me.

Curling my arm closer toward myself without tipping over the plates, I shook my head. "Not for you. The prisoners. If they don't eat properly, Domitia will not have any leverage to worry about down there."

"Go ahead." He stepped aside, opening the door, and I didn't hesitate venturing down. Out of all the guards, that particular one was giving me leniency, and for a newcomer, it was strange.

Ashroy paced in the tight quarters of his cell as he listened to one of Edda's numerous stories. I assumed they were many because every time she wasn't sleeping, she was spinning a tale. When he realized I was approaching, he paused and caught my gaze.

I slid the plates into their confines and offered the smallest smile to Edda. Over the past week, she'd grown uncertain of me, largely because I'd needed to show my fealty to Domitia and beat Ashroy. He'd understood and only nodded to me before enduring a knee to the stomach and a punch that split his lip.

It had pleased her enough, but there was no pleasure in it for me. After that incident, I respected Ashroy a little more, but Edda had grown frightened.

"How did you manage a real breakfast?" Ashroy asked as he bent to take his and slid Edda her plate. "With forks?"

"The cook doesn't care, and there is a new guard I don't recognize. I find it strange they saw the forks and didn't take them away. Between picking a lock or using it to stab someone—"

"That is odd." Ashroy, despite living in filth, lifted his fork and ate slowly. Even Edda had thrown her etiquette out the window and made quick work of her sausage and eggs. "Domitia must not be here if you're casually strolling down to us with food."

"No, she's out meeting her arriving forces. They're not grand in size, a small scouting group at best."

"Shit," Ashroy muttered.

Abendrot's army could squash them, but if she successfully garnered several other armies, I wasn't sure how the kingdom would fare. I leaned against the wall in front of their cell. "I had another dream, but this time it wasn't Stasya, it was about the Huntsmen." My voice rose in question on the name, and I winced as a throbbing pain seared through my head.

Ashroy finished his sausage and stabbed at his eggs. "That is your organization. The ones who trained you, I'm assuming. I don't know them and so I can't offer more than that, but if you're beginning to dream about other things, you're healing faster than I anticipated. This means you'd only need one round of elixir to reverse the effects of the Lethe."

I nodded and ran my hand down my face. "I could free you today," I muttered, and Edda crawled to the front of the cell. "She took a good portion of the guards with her when she left, and there are only a handful in the manor. With them dispersed . . ."

"It could be a trap," Ashroy offered and glanced down at Edda. "Do you think it's worth the risk?"

I wasn't certain.

"Let me come up with a plan, and if Domitia returns, we'll have an answer." I started to turn away, but Edda reached her hand through the rungs. Stopping, I moved closer and cocked my head. "Yes, little mite?"

She wrinkled her nose at the nickname I'd conjured up for her. "Thank you for trying." I squatted down in front of her and was struck, not for the first time, by how much she reminded me of Liesel.

I took her hand and squeezed it. "I'll get you out of here."

And I would, but I wasn't sure what it would cost me.

It turned out, I didn't have to wait long to make a decision. The sun was just starting to go down when one of the guards noticed movement outside. And by movement, he meant someone was advancing on the manor.

"You." The self-proclaimed captain pointed at me. "Take half of the men around the back for an ambush. We'll remain in the house to guard the prisoners and form the last line of defense. Got it?"

"Do I get a weapon?"

The guard scoffed. "I'm not an idiot." Yes he was, if he trusted me enough to be alone with half his men.

I shrugged. "See you on the other side." I mock saluted him and left the front hall, collecting the other half of the guards as we made our way to the back of the manor.

Snow crunched beneath my boots as I rounded the corner, and my breath billowed from me in visible clouds. Flakes clung to my lashes, then melted and streamed down my face.

"Well fuck, it's the crown princess," one of the men by me said, and I followed his line of sight to the unmistakable head of ivory hair. She sat atop a horse, watching as her men tore through the first line of defense. We'd be the second if we rushed forward, but that wasn't going to happen.

A strong urge to protect Stasya at all costs rose up in me. I couldn't let them be ambushed, and I'd stop it from happening.

While the guards around me watched, waiting for the signal to advance, I elbowed the nearest one, and he loosened his hold on the sword in his grasp enough so I could knock it free. Ducking low, I picked it up and dealt a killing blow to his neck. His comrades immediately spun on me.

I needed one alive. One to make this look as though the rescue party had done it and not me. I wasn't going to join Edda and Ashroy—as long as Domitia had me, they would be safe for the time being.

As a guard rushed at me, I squatted low and took him out at the hips. When he flipped over, I whirled around and embedded the sword in his chest. He didn't flail for long. With two down, there were six more to go.

Just when I rose to my full height, the tip of a sword grazed my cheek, and I turned on the man, knocking his blade to the side with my own. The others converged on me, and I had to rely on muscle memory of what I, apparently, knew.

One of them stumbled over a fallen guard, and I spun toward them, burying my sword into their abdomen once, twice, and as I yanked it free, I thrust the blade forward at an approaching guard.

He was larger than me in every sense and knocked away the sword in my grasp. Just as I was readying to dive forward, his boot collided with my face, stunning me. I bit the inside of my cheek, tasting blood.

Scurrying backward, I groped at the fallen guard beside me, yanked free a blade, and as my assailant lifted his sword for the killing blow, I bolted forward, embedding the dagger in his belly and twisting it.

His sword crashed down, but I was already darting toward the side. So this dance went, until there was only one guard left. I sucked in breath, then advanced. This guard was readying to flee, and I couldn't have that.

I yanked him by his collar, disarming him, then spun him around. He clocked me good in the eye, hard enough that I saw stars. Growling, I threw a punch, connecting with his jaw, and he collapsed to the ground. I pursued him, wrestling and punching.

He fought hard to live, but in the end, it wasn't enough.

My face throbbed, as did my ribs, but I'd done what I had sought to do. With one last glance toward the front yard, I watched Stasya's retinue advance on the manor, and before they could find me, I scaled the house, perched on the roof, and waited.

Six

Snow continued to fall on the land, lending the air an eerie quiet. The small party of men gathered on horseback. Their swords jutted from scabbards hanging from their saddles, and some had bows across their laps.

Someone had warned me against going with them, and that *someone* was Captain Alric, who now glowered at me from his horse. He'd told me it was foolish and unsafe, that it was something the Hawk was likely waiting for, but I ignored him. I wanted to be there for my sister. I couldn't venture inside the manor, but I could remain behind the lines and welcome her with open arms.

"Majesty, I need not remind you to remain with us at all times . . ." Alric pushed his horse through the gathering and eyed me. "It is for the good of the country, and your *sister*."

The emphasis wasn't lost on me. I pushed the hood from my head, warm breath billowing from my mouth in a cloud. "I don't need a lecture, Captain. Remember your place, and I'll remember mine."

My words encouraged an eye roll from him. "This is a mistake."

Let us hope it wasn't one that would send me into an early grave. "Is everyone ready?" When Alric nodded in response, I lifted my head and motioned everyone on.

I caught sight of a black wolf with green eyes; he peered at me, and by his side stood a smaller red wolf. Raif and Frederik.

Off we went.

It took the better part of the day to arrive on the outskirts of Lady Domitia's residence. Guards milled around the gate, behind it, and, I assumed, inside too. My men flanked the immediate area, and the wolves waited for their moment.

If I could smell Niklaus, it meant they could too. His scent was everywhere. Was he still inside?

When Alric lifted his hand, clenching his fist, they thundered forward. A flood of curses rang out as the guards at the gate readied for attack. They were ill-prepared as my men unleashed their weapons, and while the guards put up a fight, it didn't end in their favor.

Next, the men behind the iron bars turned, opening the gate quickly to take the place of their fallen comrades. Cries rang out as they lifted their swords, attempting to halt the advancement of my men.

One slipped through, advancing on me, but my horse reared, striking out. The man maneuvered around the hooves, and as my horse slipped, I leaped down from her. Relying solely on instinct, I grabbed the dagger inside my pocket and screamed as I charged forward and stabbed the man in the neck.

Blood sprayed forth, painting the snow crimson, and I stared as he fell to the ground. My ears rang, and I felt as though I'd collapse, but as Alric came into view, he took me by the shoulders.

"Stasya!" he ground out. "Are you all right?" He turned to look down at the dead man and then toward the clear path. "I'll stay with you. The others can advance with the wolves."

I nodded, and bile rose, forcing me to turn away from Alric and spew. He said something, but I didn't hear, and then he grabbed my mare's reins, soothing her.

All I could do was watch as the wolves ran around the back of the home, then reappeared before heading inside with the small party of guards. As the soldiers and wolves burst into the home, the sound of snarls and cries of anguish filled the air.

"I can't just stand here," I said, longing to bolt inside the house. But I was no warrior, and though I'd asked Alric to show me how to protect myself, I wasn't sure how I'd fare with a battle-seasoned opponent.

Alric grunted. "You will because you are Abendrot's ruler, our soon-to-be queen, and if you were to die, you'd be playing into Lady Domitia's plans."

Damn him for making sense.

Time ticked by, one minute after the other, until I was certain something had happened to my team. Just when I couldn't endure it any longer, I saw one of the men exit the manor with a smaller individual tucked into his side. I'd recognize that wild head of hair anywhere.

"Edda!" I shouted and ran forward, pushing through the wrought-iron gate, charging through the snow. "Oh my gods, Edda."

"Stasya?" Edda sobbed as she moved away from the guard.

"Edda!" I closed the distance between us, wrapping my arms around her. She was filthy and smelled of must and body odor. But she was alive, and she was well enough. "I've been sick over you." I refused to let her go. Both of our bodies trembled as we sobbed.

"We need to move now," Alric ordered.

Behind Edda, Ashroy met my gaze. His hair wasn't the stark blond I remembered. It was a dingy gray, and instead of being slicked back, it hung in limp strings around his face, which was now coated in a fine stubble. Bruises purpled his fair skin, and dark bags circled beneath his eyes.

"She is a survivor. No doubt she gets that from you." Ashroy smiled, bowing his head slightly. He looked worse than Edda. An ugly bruise marred his jaw, and judging by the way he spoke, it hurt.

I wasn't about to let go of Edda, but when I spoke over her head, I locked eyes with him. "Whatever hand you had in her wellbeing, thank you." I pried Edda from myself so I could mount my horse. As Edda reached for me, I gripped her hands and pulled her into the saddle before me. "Thank you, Ashroy." My arms encircled my sister, and I swore to never let go.

Ashroy joined one soldier in the saddle, his body sagging. "Don't thank me yet. We have a serious problem." He turned to look over his shoulder, and I wondered what he was searching for. Was it Niklaus?

Raif returned to us, hidden behind a horse, likely for my and Edda's benefit. "There were guards taken out behind the manor, and it wasn't done by us." His lips thinned, and he nodded to me as if reading my thoughts. "Either they were planted, or it was Niklaus."

"It was him," Ashroy offered with the faintest of smiles. "He said he would help us, and I think that was his way."

I lifted my gaze, looking to the roof, expecting Niklaus there with how easily he could scale buildings, and how he'd done it so often at the castle, but no one was there.

IT WAS LATE when we returned home, and I promised Ashroy I'd speak to him as soon as Edda was comfortable. He had told us what he knew of Lady Domitia and praised us for being clever.

My sister was my priority. She had several weeks of filth to remove, and knots had formed in her hair, which was in desperate need of cutting. By the time she was cleaned and dressed, she resembled the bubbly girl I remembered, but there were shadows beneath her eyes and a haunted look in her gaze. I couldn't blame her.

She wasn't willing to part from my side, so we all gathered in the dining hall for a late supper to discuss what we knew.

Ashroy had cleaned up but hadn't bothered to style his hair; it fell in pale blond waves that tickled his high cheekbones. He'd tidied his facial hair but left the growing shadow there, which made him look older. Unfortunately, remnants of his imprisonment were still visible in the sores around his wrists and the choker around his neck. I wondered how we'd be able to take it off.

"I didn't mean to delay our conversation. I thought everyone would feel better after bathing and eating." I motioned to the food before us and sat down. "What were you saying before we journeyed back?"

"Your beloved wolf-boy, he doesn't remember the current events. It appears everything from the time of his meeting you has been forgotten. Niklaus, of course, knows you are the crown princess and knew who Edda was." Color rushed to my ears and painted my cheeks red. I didn't retort. I let him finish. "I thought he was interesting before, but it turns out Niklaus is even more interesting when he remembers nothing. He *really* isn't a fan of the royal family." Ashroy turned his crystalline gaze on me and smiled. "Lucky for us all, he's fairly reasonable when he's not trying to kill you." Ashroy took up a buttered roll and bit into it.

"Ashroy said he'd remember, *eventually*," Edda added. "And he remembers fractions. They're coming to him little by little."

"He will. But the interesting thing is this: When Domitia wasn't around, he'd waltz down to our holding cells and terrorize me, or so the guards thought. I found it interesting that Domitia allows Niklaus to roam, but make no mistake about it, he is tethered." Ashroy bowed his head, taking a break from speaking to shovel food into his mouth. This time, it was without grace.

"Sometimes he'd talk to me too. He'd ask me questions about you," Edda said through a mouthful of pork.

I clenched my fists as she spoke, not wanting to think about how he'd forgotten me. About how he was butchering my kingdom.

Ashroy broke a piece of bread apart before continuing. "During our exchanges, he'd listen to me, and I could *see* him warring with what I said. Stasya, Nik would relay messages for me to Ishkertov. I've been getting responses in return. Whatever you may think, you're not alone, and Ishkertov has Abendrot's back. And more than that—we're ready. Our alliances are waiting for the word. I don't know what you've heard or done in our absence—"

I set my fork down, tears pooling in my eyes. Tears of relief I refused to shed. "Thank you," I whispered. I waited a beat before gathering my resolve. "I've reached out to our alliances too, and we've patched up some hard feelings. I opened more trade lines with them, which is mutually beneficial, and they're offering help with small forces from their army."

Ashroy's eyebrows lifted in surprise, and a warm smile turned the corner of his lips up. "I am impressed, Your Highness. Although, I shouldn't be . . . Tenacity runs in the family." His eyes slid to Edda, who smiled and laughed. "I'm glad to know this, it'll help our advances. Lady Domitia is out meeting her own arriving forces, at least some of them."

I took a long sip of the wine in front of me and shook my head. "Did he truly beat you every time you spoke?"

Ashroy wiped his mouth and let his stomach rest, a wry smile replacing the confident one. "No. Only when he needed to, and I understood." He sighed. "Lethe can't erase memories, not entirely. It isn't like removing them, it's more just blurring them. Each night, he'd be plagued with half-memories, or *dreams* as he'd call them. He knows that I know him and that I know the truth. So, when he roughed me up to save face, he'd ask me to clarify. I told him I would, but for a price. Initially, he didn't take it, but eventually, he came back and was willing to pay."

"Is that why he delivered the letters for you?" I asked.

"Indeed. Something bothered him at night and was driving him mad, but he wasn't sure what. He didn't want to believe me at first, but when what he felt aligned with what I said, he knew I wasn't lying."

"So, there is hope." I felt my spirits lifting, and a small smile tugged at my lips, but it was premature.

Ashroy bent his head and rubbed at his eye. "Even so. He is not who you knew before. And if by some chance he storms into this castle, *don't* think otherwise. He's conflicted and confused. But I don't pretend to know how to predict him, Stasya."

How did that differ from before? Except I knew I could trust Niklaus then, I knew that he wouldn't purposely hurt me. I remembered the way he stared me down, threatened my family if we didn't change. "That is the version walking around now? From before everything?"

"More or less, maybe worse. His body still remembers how to fight, but his mind recalls hatred, which is easily molded by a mastermind. Enter: Lady Domitia. She's twisting his memories and making things more difficult."

Ashroy must have seen my discomfort because he reached out and let his hand rest on top of mine. "Difficult, but not impossible. As I told him, the bond will make things easier."

I nodded and left it at that. Ashroy deserved to eat in peace and relax now that he was safe. Everyone else at the table rapidly fired questions at him, and I half listened.

After everyone had had their fill, they left for the evening, leaving me alone with Ashroy.

"I'm so glad that you're all right. I kept thinking the worst things, and Edda . . ." My eyes drifted to the hollow of his throat. Instead of skin, I saw the ugly collar that rendered his magic useless.

Ashroy turned away from the fireplace, the flames' shadows dancing against his face. He followed my line of sight and touched the thick necklace. "She is strong, and she loves you very much." He walked the distance between us and embraced me. "The thought of you fighting kept her spirits high." His lips pressed a soft kiss to my temple, and when he pulled back, his eyes drifted to my lips. Ashroy dipped his head, and I didn't move, knowing what would come next. His lips connected with mine in a soft kiss that ended as quickly as it began.

My cheeks flushed at once. I didn't feel the burning desire I would have with Niklaus—I felt nothing. Ashroy didn't repulse me, but he also didn't stir feelings. I said nothing as he stared at me, perhaps hoping I'd speak.

"I mean no harm," he finally said. "I know you're unavailable, and I've known that since I arrived. I'm here as a friend, as an ally. As Ishkertov and myself."

When the shock faded, I gathered my wits. I needed all the allies I could get. "Then let's formulate a plan for when Niklaus comes knocking, because it's only a matter of time before Lady Domitia sends him our way. We also need to figure out how to remove that from you."

"Of course. Who needs sleep, anyway?" Ashroy grinned. "As for this—" He pointed at his neck and sighed. "Domitia will need to remove it, or she'll need to die."

"I rather like the idea of her dying," I said coldly.

Ashroy chuckled. "I thought you might." He walked to the table and retrieved my goblet of wine. "So, let's plot." He raised his goblet, and in turn, I raised mine, clinking it against the other.

Seven

ow that Edda was home and Ashroy was back, it
was time to confront the fact that there was only
one remaining Council member: Lord Aksel. And why
he hadn't been picked off yet, I wasn't certain.

"Five people on the Council have died. Good gods,
Stasya!" Lord Aksel shouted at me, jamming his fingers
through his faded red hair. "And you're just going to let
this happen?" He paced back and forth, nearly foaming
at the mouth.

"Don't be ridiculous, and don't forget who you're
speaking to. What more can I do? I have sent soldiers to
guard members, on top of their own security too. And
that did *nothing*." I stood behind my chair, watching him
carefully. He stalked back and forth like a caged animal.
No doubt he felt cornered and ready to lash out. But
how could *he* thwart the threat when he didn't even
know who, or where, his enemy was?

Certainly, Niklaus was the one eradicating the Council, but there was more at play, more of a threat than a puppet of an assassin.

"When your Council is empty, they'll come for you. It'll be your head on a pike next." Lord Aksel barely got his words out before Alric rounded the corner and took him by the shoulders to force him into the chair.

Alric bent at the waist and lifted a finger. "Mind your tongue, and remember that is *your* future queen."

My lips twitched as Alric took matters into his own hands. Lord Aksel wasn't a terrible man, and I agreed with him on most matters. When my father had turned a blind eye to reason, Lord Aksel had done his best to convince my father it was *wrong*. However, fear was a master manipulator, and it could poison even the most resolute mind.

"I respect you, Lord Aksel, including your concerns and opinions. Short of stepping into a field with my arms held out wide, I don't know what to do. My people are being run in circles because this is a game to *her*." It was true, mostly.

We wanted Domitia and her allies to think we were mindlessly following them around and around again. We *had been* to begin with, but no more. We would not play into their hands; it was their turn to come to us. Ashroy assured me that war would not come to Abendrot, and that his alliances were waiting. I didn't want to put all my trust in him, but I had no choice. No one else was here to help me or the kingdom.

Lord Aksel gazed up at me, his bushy brows furrowing. "So, that's it? We give up, and I'm next to die? They will slaughter my family alongside me, and Abendrot will belong to the invisible foe." He dragged a hand down his face and shook his head. "No. I won't stand for that."

I couldn't promise he'd live through this, or even that I would. "Neither will I. We will get through this together. Your family will prosper with you, Lord Aksel. If it takes me standing in the field, that's what I'll do to end all of this madness."

Alric's lips pressed into a thin line. I knew at once that he wanted to disagree with me, but Lord Aksel shook his head and stood from the chair. "No. I'll trust you and those that are working on this matter."

"Somehow, we will put an end to this."

"We can hope," Lord Aksel said. There was no fire in his words as he spoke them, only the same exhaustion we all felt. "Be well, Your Majesty." He bowed and backed out of the room, leaving Alric and me to the silence.

"Please tell me you aren't considering using yourself as bait," Alric broke the silence. He moved from the shadows he'd clung to moments ago and approached me from behind. "You are the future of this kingdom, and while I know I need not remind you of that, I can't help but feel as though you're withholding something from me. I swore an oath to protect the crown at all costs—I believe it's my right to know what I'm getting myself into. Especially if it means my life."

Tears of anger and stress pooled in my eyes. I swiped

angrily at them and shifted my jaw. "I don't want you to give your life for mine."

"Too bad." He turned his palms toward me and shrugged unapologetically. "I want your honesty, that's all."

"Niklaus is coming here next. Names that I can't speak heard chatter in the woods, and in a few days, there will be new recruits for guards in the castle. Except they aren't—they're part of the Huntsmen."

Alric stared hard, then scrunched his face up and pinched the bridge of his nose. "Were you going to tell me this at all?" Silence met his question. "Dammit. How am I supposed to keep you safe if I don't know things?"

"Fair enough. I'm sorry." I truly was. I didn't enjoy withholding information, but the fewer people that knew, the better. "Frederik has been staying here because he and Raif will take Niklaus down. They're the only ones who can if he decides he doesn't *want* to be caught."

Alric grew quiet, his facial muscles tightening. He didn't need to say a word. I had grown to know him well enough and knew he would have preferred to put an arrow in Niklaus' heart. I hoped it wouldn't come to that.

"A few days. Nothing more accurate than that?" he mused out loud.

"No. We wait."

"You don't need a damn field—you've got the castle." Alric groaned, then walked to the table to slam his fist down. "I'll take him down if I have to." That was his job, and I wasn't about to berate him for it.

This wasn't an easy thing for him to swallow, knowing I was endangering myself and not able to stop it. I closed the distance between us and wrapped my arms around his waist. He stiffened at first, then relaxed when I squeezed harder.

"You didn't sign up for any of this. You are an honorable man, and I know every fiber in you detests Niklaus. So know this: I appreciate you, and over the past few months, I can honestly say that I've grown to love you as one would an uncle."

His shoulders slumped as I spoke, and when I finished, he turned around to grab my shoulders. "That would explain why you infuriate me. A bull-headed niece who refuses to listen to her elder." Alric grinned weakly but winked. "I will do my best to abide by this, Stasya. On my word."

"That is all I expect, Alric."

THE DAY after Lord Aksel met with me, Ashroy questioned our plan to draw Niklaus out. He had second thoughts and was visibly on edge. *Everyone* was on edge, including me. I was a hair's breadth away from snapping at the next person to question what I was doing because the truth was, I didn't know. I wondered if my father had known what *he* was doing at every turn, or if he, like me, only did his best.

"Stasya, you infiltrated Lady Domitia's domain, do you think she will play nicely this time around?" Ashroy kept his voice low, but his crystal gaze locked onto mine.

"We're running out of options, aren't we?" I snapped. My fingers balled into fists as I walked up to him. The last thing I wanted to do was destroy a friendship, or worse, an alliance. But we were out of options.

His eyes flicked toward the nearby window. "I'm exploring other options. I just—I don't . . ."

"You don't trust him, I know. No one does."

"That isn't fair!" Ashroy hissed. "I learned my fair share about him while they held me captive. The only thing that will save you is your bond. Everything hangs in the balance over that *bond*."

I growled, a half-human, half-animal sound. My hand moved faster than my mind could process. I struck his face, and I didn't realize what I'd done until Ashroy was staring at me with barely restrained fury. In his eyes, I saw hurt too. Before I could say anything or apologize, he stormed off without a word.

Every muscle, every fiber in my being yearned to stretch and to grow until I was a hulking wolf. I wanted to run as fast as I could until my limbs and lungs burned. Yet here I was, a prisoner in the castle yet again. If I could distance myself from this place for even a little while, I'd be able to breathe.

I sat outside in the garden, twisting a dead branch between my forefinger and thumb. The dead of winter was upon us, either blanketing the ground in snow or encasing everything in ice. Cool air wafted against my skin, attempting to chill me, but the heat beneath my flesh diminished its strength. I tossed the branch down and stood from the stone bench to walk around the bushes-turned-ice-sculptures. Reaching out, I flicked a piece of ice off.

A hand rested on my shoulder. I spun around, air seizing in my lungs, and stared at the wide-eyed face before me. My heart galloped wildly in my chest as I reached out to cup Edda's face. "Don't scare me like that," I wheezed.

I should have heard her, but I was so lost in my head that I hadn't. *Foolish*, I thought.

"Ashroy told me you were in quite the state," Edda said. She reached up to clasp my wrist with both hands. "Are you all right?"

How could my sister be asking me this? When she was the one who had been imprisoned, fed scraps of food, and made to hear the guards gloat of every victory.

"Me?" I pressed my forehead to hers and closed my eyes. "Yes, I'm fine."

"Don't do that. Don't lie to me." Edda backed up enough so she could look me in the eye. "It's okay to not be all right, but it's not okay to lie about being fine. This whole situation is awful—all of it. But I'm here, and so are Raif, Frederik, Ashroy. Gods, Stasya! You have so many people here for you. Don't push them away, especially when you need them."

At her words, I shied away. Not from hurt, no—I

stood there and admired my younger sister, who was becoming such a wise young lady. Edda had the heart of a lion and the soul of an ancient.

"You're growing up too fast," I said. "You also look like you're freezing. Let's go inside, and we can drink some hot cider in my room. I think it's time we talk, and truly *talk*."

Edda nodded, then pressed against my side as we walked back inside. I could pull myself together for Edda, and I would, because we both needed one another's company.

After sending for dinner and two flagons of hot cider upstairs, Edda and I ventured to my suite. The hearth was kept blazing out of habit, which Edda seemed grateful for.

"The food and drink should be up soon." I walked to the bookshelf against the wall and took out a book, smiling to myself. "Remember when I used to read this to you *all* the time? About the cursed prince who became a giant fox and *ate* people?"

"I loved that story. They viewed Princess Gisela as a weakling because she was sick," Edda said, crossing the room to take the red leather-bound book from my grasp. She opened to an illustrated page. A fox hovered above a young woman, baring his teeth, but she stood resolute with her hand held outward. "Gisela was frightened by him, but she was tired of the fox destroying her people. Even though she was terrified, she opted to sacrifice herself for the greater good." Edda flipped through a few more pages, settling on one of my favorites: a picture of the fox covered in burs and briars. "The fox made demands of the princess that even a servant would gripe about." Edda paused and looked at me.

I took the bait and continued for her. "All the princess required was for the fox to ask nicely. After a while, he did. It was her inner strength and kindness that ended up breaking the curse . . . and also her love for the brutish fox."

Edda lifted her eyebrows pointedly.

Unable to think of a clever remark, I scoffed. "I guess there is no point in reading it if we know it by heart." I crossed the room and sat at the small table by the fireplace, staring into the flickering flames. "We haven't had a lot of time to be alone since your return. Please talk to me."

She was quiet for a moment, then she pushed me over in the chair and pressed against my side. "There isn't much to say outside of what you know. It was terrifying, and I missed you. I never knew what was coming —if they would kill me or hurt me." Sighing, Edda wrapped her arms around me. "Ashroy kept me sane, and in his way, he kept me safe too. He took the brunt of everything. He gave me most of his food, unless Niklaus brought us full portions." Her voice broke at the end of her words. "I don't want to talk about it anymore, honestly. I want to heal. I want to feel normal."

The sound of Edda's voice as she spoke made my heart tighten, and tears pooled in my eyes. If I could have switched places with her, I would have. "All right. I want to know about the twinkle you get in your eye every time you look at or talk about Ashroy." I teased, but it was enough to allow both of us to relax.

When we were too tired to talk and full from supper, we decided it was time to sleep. Edda kissed my cheek and hugged me tightly before disappearing down the hall. However, it wasn't so easy for me. Alric showed up, accompanied by Raif and Frederik. The three of them stared at me, but it was Alric who spoke up.

"Tonight, it would be best for the boys to remain in your room. If an attempt is made on your life, they are more capable than me." I guessed those words were hard for him to swallow, but he said them with no bite.

Raif smiled at me, but Frederik had a hard time maintaining eye contact. "Is it the only way . . . ?" I sighed, looking between the three of them.

"I'm sorry, Stasya, but it's the only option I'm comfortable with. Now that we know Niklaus isn't in his best form—" Alric cleared his throat as if battling a smart-mouthed remark.

My jaw clenched as he failed to finish his words. "Very well. If they're to stay in my room, they need appropriate bedding. Have someone fetch more pillows and blankets for them. They're not going to just sit in a chair all night."

Raif signed a "thank you."

"Of course. I suppose we should get situated inside, then." So much for sleeping tonight.

A servant brought in a spare chair and ottoman, so Raif and Frederik each had one to curl up with. Once they made themselves comfortable, I crawled into bed still wearing the dress I had on for the day. Sleep wouldn't visit me tonight, so a book for company sounded divine. Pulling it from the nightstand, I opened the page, then jumped at the sound of Frederik's voice. I hadn't forgotten he was there, but the sudden noise amongst the silence startled me.

"Can you read to me?" Frederik asked.

"Read to you?" I echoed his question and smiled, flicking the pages of the book open. "This story is about a goddess who was tricked by her sister and cast out of the heavens. Does that interest you?"

Frederik turned in the chair and faced me. "Mm-hmm."

So, I read the book to Frederik—or at least, I would have had I not fallen asleep in the middle of it.

EIGHT

I woke to the sound of snarls. Frederik and Raif had tackled someone to the ground. Sleep fogged my mind, but when I sprang up and flew backward from the bed, I made out the individual on the floor, who thrashed like a trapped animal. It was Niklaus.

He growled and did his best to kick the others away, but Frederik and Raif were werewolves too, and their added strength kept him in place. I zeroed in on the weapon within Niklaus' reach—a crossbow—just as Raif grabbed it and tossed it aside.

Alric barged into the room. His foot kicked away the crossbow, which had clattered to the ground, and his eyes hardened as he peered down at Niklaus. "Quit your wiggling around. You're not going anywhere."

"You need to let me go," Niklaus snarled. "Keeping me here will put an arrow in all of your heads." His eyes tore away from his captors and focused on me. "I'm not here to kill you."

Then why the crossbow? My heart, which had been thundering faster than a galloping horse, slowed a fraction. "Is that so? You could have fooled me. You came through my window with a weapon—a loaded one, at that." I motioned to the crossbow, which had a bolt already secured in place. "Don't come here and lie to me."

"I'm not lying," Niklaus replied, his fighting ceasing. He gazed up at the other two and grumbled, "I came here to warn you."

I looked to Alric, and he nodded, removing a pair of manacles from his hip. He opened them and secured Niklaus' wrists behind his back. Frederik and Raif stood on either side of him, ready to force him back down if need be. As much as it pained me to see Niklaus in irons, it was a necessity.

"If you're not here to kill me like you have my Council, tell me why you *are* here, Niklaus von Brandt." I lifted a hand to rest over my heart, feeling the now calm and steady thrum.

He grinned from his kneeling position on the floor and laughed. "If I wanted you dead, *princess,* you would be. Your beloved captain would never have gotten the irons on me. And your wolf friends would have bolts in their hearts."

Frederik flinched but didn't say anything.

Anger sparked inside my chest. I crossed the distance between us, hovering over Niklaus. His lips twisted into a confident grin, and his devilish yellow eyes twinkled with something that looked like triumph. Narrowing my eyes, I lifted my hand and struck him across the face with a satisfying *smack*. "That is for leaving me without saying goodbye and for having the audacity to sneak through my window. I don't know what your game is with that bitch of a woman, Niklaus, but it ends now." I seethed, nearly shaking with fury.

The commotion must have spread through the castle like wildfire because Ashroy burst through my door in the next moment. "This surely isn't the reunion any of us were planning, is it?" He stood beside me, hair ruffled and robe loosely tied around himself.

"Look who it is, the princeling," Niklaus said, but it held little bite to it. In fact, he seemed more annoyed with me than Ashroy.

Ashroy glanced in my direction and then back at Niklaus. "Did you hit him?" I nodded. "Good on you. Maybe you should do it again and see if it'll rattle any memories."

"As I recall, you owe me a few good ones, princeling." Niklaus' lips twisted into a grin.

Ashroy shrugged, then waved a hand in the air. "You're lacking your usual wit. What's the matter, a bird caught your tongue?"

Niklaus visibly tensed, but he didn't say anything. Alric shoved him downward until his chest pressed against the stone floor. This time, he did fight against the pressure.

"I have ninety-nine problems, but a lack of wit isn't one of them," Niklaus said through a throaty laugh.

"Well, why are you here, Nik?" Ashroy sounded perturbed. "I know it was you who took out the guards. You promised to help Edda and me, which you did . . . What did Domitia do to you?"

Whatever was going on between the two of them could wait. "Let him up. For gods' sake, let him up and sit him down on the bed. Since we're all having a meeting in my private suite, make yourselves comfortable." I spun on my heel, refusing to sit until they were all situated. Stubbornly, none of them moved. "Sit him down on the bed!" They complied this time.

Niklaus sat on my bed and looked unsure, his eyes trained on the floor as he waited for the inevitable question.

"Why are you here?" I asked slowly.

Time ticked on between us, and tension built in the air. "I . . . I saw you at the manor. When you arrived, while I don't remember anything with us . . . I felt it. The urge to protect you, to stop the guards from advancing on you." He swore none too quietly and looked so torn. "I needed to see you again," Niklaus offered quietly.

My brows furrowed, then my nose wrinkled as I puzzled over his answer. "Why?"

"Because you're haunting my dreams. Everything is, but you especially." His voice was rough, and for the first time, I noticed the dark circles beneath his eyes. This could be a game, but Niklaus had never feigned desperation before, and there was a very strained quality to his voice.

Heat rushed into my cheeks. Niklaus lifted his eyes and stared at me. There was no smirk, no smile, just a blank *expression*. This conversation was taking a personal twist, and I didn't want any of the current audience privy to it. "Everyone out."

"I don't think—" Ashroy started.

"What!?" Alric shouted at the same time.

I glanced between Ashroy and Alric. "Everyone out. If you feel as though it's a poor decision, which I know it is, hand me a weapon and I'll use it on him."

"No, I refuse to leave you with him." Alric stood firm, and I couldn't blame him.

Frustrated, I glanced around my room and motioned toward my bedpost. "Chain him to the bed."

Alric grumbled, pulling a dagger from his belt. "Don't make me regret this, Highness." He handed me the blade and set to securing Niklaus in place. It was an awkward position because he had to sit on the bed with his back against the post, but he didn't complain.

With one last curse, Alric motioned for everyone to follow him out of the room. "We'll be outside the door."

Once the door closed, I stood a good distance away from Niklaus. "That's because we're mates." I still didn't trust him. He wasn't *my* Niklaus.

His body sagged, not in defeat, but exhaustion was my guess. "She sent me here to kill you, but I knew I wouldn't—that I couldn't. She doesn't know what you are to me, and because of that, she doesn't know that I'd never be able to accomplish that mission." Niklaus closed his eyes. The firelight cast strange shadows over his freckled face. "I don't remember any of it—not that I remember much. I've tried until I thought my head would crack open. But I feel it inside, the thrum and the bond we share, and it haunts me in my dreams."

At first, I didn't want to move, but eventually, I crept forward until I sat next to him. I put the dagger on my lap and watched his expressions flicker through his eyes. Emptiness, longing, confusion, and anger. As far as I knew, Niklaus had never been able to feel, let alone express his emotions well.

"I understand why you left without saying goodbye, and I know you don't remember doing it, but gods, I hate you for doing that." I gritted my teeth, trying to hold back my own emotions, not because I was ashamed but because I wanted to finish my train of thought. "No arrow could hurt more than that."

"Domitia's forces won't ever make it here," Niklaus offered, interrupting the moment. "She's been having difficulty convincing them to step into enemy territory, mainly because Ishkertov's alliances are following through with Ashroy's plans." He paused and cocked his head. "I'm assuming he told you."

"He did."

Niklaus allowed his body to fall backward onto the bed. He shifted his arms so he could rest comfortably and closed his eyes. "Without the support and her numbers dwindling, it's only a matter of time before she's defeated. She's fighting a losing battle."

Ishkertov was the largest country on our continent, and if their forces weren't enough, their strong alliances would be. Long ago, we'd shared many, but as my father broke treaties throughout the years, we lost our footholds.

Thank the gods for Ashroy.

I gripped the dagger and placed it on the bed beside me before I twisted around and crawled toward Niklaus. "Please tell me you're in there somewhere. That beyond the clouded memories, you truly remember me," I whispered as I leaned over his face.

When he opened his eyes, it was a stranger's gaze. Somewhere beyond those eyes was my Niklaus. He leaned forward and caught my lips in a kiss. It wasn't gentle or soft, but it was deep and probing. I groaned in response, tasting him as our tongues clashed in a heated dance. His hands were bound, but mine weren't, and I took full advantage of that. They roamed over his muscled chest, tingling as they recalled the feel of his hard muscles and warm skin.

Niklaus' long legs twisted around mine, trying to trap me there. His raspy chuckle into my mouth washed over every inch of me. That was *my* Niklaus. My hands roamed up his shoulders and into his wayward red locks, where I tugged them with little care. He growled softly as he pulled away and breathed heavily against my neck. Rough hair tickled my neck. He'd grown a short beard since the last time I'd seen him.

"I think I like the idea of this," I murmured.

"Me unable to touch you?" His voice almost cracked.

"It's a terrible, evil idea." His head leaned against the post as he closed his eyes. "I remember that. Not while I'm awake, but when I drift off to sleep. That's when the memories come back. And by morning, they're gone except for wisps." Niklaus shook his head, sighing.

I looked down at him. Playfulness aside, to see him treated like this poured salt into my wounds. "I am here, Niklaus, right where you left me. Safe, remember?" My voice cracked as the last words tumbled from my lips. "I will unlock those, but we need to talk."

"Why would you . . . ?"

It was stupid. Unsafe. And I was certain Alric would ream me out for it, but I had to trust that Niklaus was in there somewhere.

I scooted off the bed and pulled a decorative pin from my vanity before turning Niklaus around. "I'm sure this will work," I said, half to myself. With Niklaus' back facing me, I set to work on the irons. Sliding the slender hair piece into the lock mechanism, I twisted it, feeling for the latch, and fiddled for a moment or two until they clicked open.

"Someone has had a lot of practice," Niklaus offered. In a blink, he discarded the manacles and grabbed me by the wrists, yanking me into his lap. "We can talk after," he murmured drowsily against my chest.

I didn't want to be the sensible one. I didn't want to pull away, not when every fiber of my being yearned to unite with him. It was an odd predicament to be caught in. I felt as though I was being untrue to *my* Niklaus. But as his lips dragged downward and his strong fingers tugged my hips against his body, my sensibilities went out the window.

Niklaus' gestures weren't rough. They were tender as they had been our last time together. Every teasing brush of his fingers set new nerves on fire that only cooled as he began peeling the fabric away from my body. I ran my fingers beneath the hem of his shirt and lifted it over his head, throwing it to the side without a care. My fingers explored his freckled skin, and I knew no matter how hard I tried, I'd never be able to count them.

I gasped as his mouth covered my neck. My eyes slammed shut as I recalled our bond snapping into place. "This time, you're staying." That was the last word I uttered before our clothes met their fate on the floor and our bodies collided.

Thank the gods that the doors were thick enough to mute my cries and when I was on the verge of growing too loud, Niklaus covered my lips with his. The last thing I wanted was Alric barging in. And as Niklaus fingers bit into the curve of my bottom, everything but us faded away.

Afterward, I dared not close my eyes and instead, I propped my head up so I could gaze down at the devil in my bed. "Is it true what you said? That it's only a waiting game now?"

Niklaus rolled onto his side to face me, one eyebrow quirked in question. "Somewhat. She'll fight as she goes down, make no mistake about that. She will pull every trick she has up her sleeve."

His words echoed in my ears. "Niklaus, is she a witch?" A raspy laugh tickled my ears. Even though he was laughing at me, it warmed my belly.

"No, why would you think that?"

"She uses magic frequently," I offered. "Alric told me she used it on you before, and then there is Ashroy's enchanted choker. The Lethe . . ."

Niklaus closed his eyes, relaxing into the comfort of the pillows and bed. "It's one of her tricks. She uses people like stepping stones, and if they expire during their task, so be it. Lethe is less magic and more herbalism." His words trailed off as sleep threatened to pull him under.

"But what about you?" He didn't answer immediately, and I thought he wouldn't, that he'd fallen asleep. But then he sighed, shrugging his shoulders.

"I'm a little different. The others are stones, but me? Consider me a pet. If I step out of line, I'm punished. And if I'm good, I'm praised."

Questions flooded my mind. How was he praised and how was he punished? My face heated in anger, and by the time I collected myself, Niklaus had succumbed to exhaustion and snored softly. There was no way I'd be falling back asleep tonight, so instead, I absorbed his company for the brief time we had.

Shortly after he fell asleep, Alric entered the room. I wasn't in my bed but curled up in one of the chairs in the room, reading.

Alric took one glance at the bed, then me, and glared. I lifted a finger to my lips, shushing him, but it didn't stop him from approaching me.

"You undid his bindings?" His jaw muscle worked. "I'm sending for Raif and Frederik, since you have a death wish."

Perhaps that was a little true and maybe I was a touch mad to believe Niklaus, for not distancing myself from him. So, I didn't argue with Alric.

Frederik and Raif entered, took up their respective posts, and so went the night.

COME MORNING, I'd already dressed for the day when Elka entered the room. She glanced at the bed first, saw Niklaus, and screamed. This startled all three of the males, pulling them from their slumber.

"Elka, peace, it's okay!" I rushed toward her, but not before the guards flooded the room. Alric was the first to burst in, and when he saw nothing was out of sorts, he relaxed, but the guards remained with us.

Raif and Frederik settled but were on their feet, no doubt shaking off the sudden rush of adrenaline.

Niklaus had sprung from the bed, annoyance clear on his face, but he didn't say a word. His hair was even more disheveled than usual, but paired with his new beard, it stirred a hunger in me.

"Everything is fine," I said. "Elka, you may leave." She glanced between Raif and myself, then left.

"With all due respect, nothing is fine, and this certainly isn't." Alric shook his head. "I offer you the suggestion of imprisoning him because either way, Lady Domitia marches toward us. At least if we lock Niklaus up, it's one less bird we have to worry about."

"I'm not one of her birds," Niklaus snapped.

"Aren't you?" Alric spat.

Niklaus shot Alric a look, but there was still a deep exhaustion that seemed to pull him down. "If you give me more time, I can stop Domitia from succeeding. I can't stop her from marching on you, but I can make a difference."

"Why should I trust you?" I asked, wondering where the words came from. Yes, I trusted him on a level, but not to the full extent I once did.

Niklaus shifted his jaw. "Because I didn't kill you, and because that means she'll find a way to punish me."

I didn't want that. Maybe locking him up was the better idea—

"Let him go," Ashroy said from the doorway and stepped forward. "I think he proved himself at the manor, killing the guards so that Edda and I could escape. Why don't we make our way to the war room instead of your private quarters, Stasya?"

"Likely the best idea." I motioned for everyone to leave, but Niklaus lingered by my vanity.

He dipped his fingers into the water and ran them

through his hair, trying to tame the wayward locks. I waited for him to join us, and the two other wolves flanked him, still not trusting he wouldn't snap.

We had work to do.

NINE

When we all sat in the meeting room, Niklaus sat farthest from me, flanked by two guards. "She won't kill me, at least not yet. She sees me as a tool, one that can break Stasya's spirit. Now that she has lost Ashroy and Edda, it's going to fall on me." Niklaus turned his head to glance in my direction. "I can convince her that killing you now isn't for the best, that the game needs to be drawn out longer, and the kingdom in near ruins. She will want to put an end to Stasya eventually, but this way, her game isn't over."

The Seidels entered the room a moment later, and although I hadn't sent for them, it was good timing on their part. I'd lost my Council—well, all but Lord Aksel —and yet here sat the roughest Council I'd ever seen in my years. My sister, the Seidels, Niklaus, Raif, Kina, Frederik, Alric, and Ashroy.

Rough but reliable.

Ashroy sipped his tea. "Just so we're clear, I'm against holding him captive."

Hope blossomed in my chest. Had Ashroy made the elixir yet? I glanced at him, but Niklaus' voice pulled me away.

"While she may not kill you, that doesn't mean she won't send someone here to capture you." Niklaus shrugged. "You'd be used against me if she knows I have a weakness for you." He paused, glancing down. "Well, she knows I do, just doesn't know that I remember."

Sabrina sighed. "But if you're already here, and it buys us some time to surround the area, is it worth it? If we're ready for the attack, and we have the Huntsmen on guard, plus the castle forces, is it worth the risk to everyone here?"

I surveyed the faces at the table. None of them seemed overly keen on the idea, and I couldn't blame them for that. Carelessly putting my life in danger wasn't at the top of my list, but if it drew in some of Domitia's lackeys and allowed for the Huntsmen to pick them off, it was the best solution.

"I don't like that idea," Niklaus ground out. "If just one person manages to get in . . ."

"Then don't let them," I retorted. "What does everyone else think?" I finally picked up a fork.

Alric slammed a fist down, attempting to talk over Lukas, who was shouting across the table at Niklaus. The chaos erupting before me did little to dissuade my appetite, and I ate while they argued. When it was clear they would not stop, I chimed in. "Enough! One at a time."

Ashroy reconsidered his initial idea. "Wolf, indeed. On second thought, I think we should keep Niklaus here and draw them out." A servant rushed into the room, bobbing a quick curtsy. She made her way to Ashroy, handed over a letter, then quickly left.

Ashroy raised a brow and broke the seal on the letter, scanning it quickly. "Yes. I definitely think we should keep him here. Our key players are in place, and they have beaten back Domitia's allies. Ishkertov is on the move, and they're not taking any prisoners." A small smile tugged at his lips. "Her alliances will crumble swiftly. No one wants to go to war with Ishkertov."

They were not only sizable but brutal when it came to warfare, and their allies were far greater than Domitia's small, and apparently dwindling, empire.

Niklaus shot him a glare. "You could have started with that, ass." He sighed, looking at me, then back to Ashroy. "Then I'll stay and let her come knocking. I don't know if she values me enough to barter, but you can try."

"This woman is stupid," Alric declared. "She wipes your memory but cannot grasp bonds—or even the human condition. If you chose Stasya once, why not again?"

The sudden outburst from the stoic captain silenced everyone.

"Perhaps she was relying on his hatred for what the crown once represented. Hate is a strong feeling. It's as strong as love and only one heartbeat away from being the same emotion." I shrugged. "All in favor of keeping Niklaus hostage, say 'aye.'"

Most of those at the table agreed, which meant he'd be housed with me in case anyone made an attempt on my life. It also meant Niklaus could reacquaint himself with me on a more intimate level.

THE DAYS PASSED FAR TOO QUICKLY for me. One morning, when I woke, Niklaus was staring down at me. Alric had allowed him in my room only when one of the other wolves was there too. The moment I met his gaze, something snapped into place: clarity. It was the warmth I felt in his embrace, the feeling of ease in his presence, and while the realization soothed me, it also petrified me. I loved Niklaus. I loved the Niklaus I knew before and the one that had his arms wrapped around me now. I loved him for his brutish qualities and the way he softened when it was needed. Over the past year that I'd known him, he'd grown by leaps and bounds. As much as he declared he could not express emotions or feel, he certainly did it well enough with me.

"Your heart is thundering away. Are you all right?" he asked, cocking his head as he sat on the edge of my bed.

"Just a bad dream," I lied. When everything was done, when we had our lives back. I'd confess everything to him—again. The words were on my tongue, ready to flow freely, but I clamped down and rested my forehead against his instead.

Niklaus lifted his hand and cupped my cheek. His thumb brushed against the skin there as his gaze held mine. "I don't know how long it'll take for me to come back, but I will, Stasya. You're not going to get rid of me that easily. Now that I know what I was missing . . ." His hand lowered to my shoulder, and his fingers played with the strap of my chemise. I wanted him to slip it off, to strip me bare, except we had an audience, and I wanted him to myself—in private.

"What were you missing?"

Niklaus shook his head and sighed. "You. My heart, my conscience." He laughed wryly and leaned down, pressing a soft kiss to the corner of my mouth. "As if the bond wasn't maddening enough, trying to muddle my way through these feelings . . ." Niklaus paused, his eyes connecting with mine.

"It wasn't easy for you before, and it won't be easy now. Maybe especially now." I turned my head to catch his lips again in a quick kiss. "What matters is that we are in it together and that we fight to keep it."

Niklaus leaned forward, capturing my lips and drawing out the desire that always seemed to surface in his presence. His hand slid along my jaw, into my mussed hair, and toward my neck, tilting my head back so he could better access my mouth. I savored his kiss, and as much as I wanted to lose myself in him, I was already withdrawing when a knock sounded on the door.

When Niklaus pulled back, Raif looked relieved for the interruption.

"My princess," Elka spoke through the door. "Are you awake? A letter has come. It's from Lady Domitia."

As soon as the wretched woman's name left Elka's lips, I sprang from the bed, grabbing my robe. "Come in."

Elka rushed in, crossing the distance between us, and handed over the letter.

Princess Stasya,

I believe you have something that belongs to me. I'm not at all fond of sharing, so if you could hand him over before I'm truly angry, I would be ever so grateful. If by chance you refuse to return my hunter, I will send a flock of hungry birds your way. They're more than willing to kill those you care about and will save you for last.

Sincerely,
The Hawk

Niklaus snorted. "There you have it. That is her bargaining: return me or die. She wants me for two reasons: because I know how to kill and because I make you weak, and in her mind, stupid."

How could paper suddenly feel as though it were crafted out of iron? I nearly dropped it as my emotions shifted from fear to anger. She thought Niklaus was her property, but he belonged to no one but *me*.

"Her threats are growing old. She means to kill me anyway so she can take my crown." I balled the paper up and tossed it across the hallway. "So what difference does it make if I speed up the process?" My voice cracked. I must have sounded hysterical to Niklaus because his eyes narrowed as he spun me around.

"Don't be stupid. No one will kill you because if I have to, I'll slaughter her entire following." His voice lowered, and his eyes, which were typically full of playfulness, hardened. Niklaus' hands came to rest on my shoulders, and he shook me. "Don't do anything idiotic. Do you understand? As much as I want to return to her so I can pick her apart from the inside, even I realize its best to remain here. She is outmanned." His eyes searched mine, and when I glanced away, his hands moved from my shoulders to my cheeks. "Dammit. Swear it, Stasya. Stay here, with me."

No part of me wanted to lie to him, but nothing in me wanted to lose Niklaus either. "All right."

"No. Say it." His jaw shifted as he patiently waited for the words he wanted to hear.

"I promise." I withdrew and looked down at the paper. "I need to share this with everyone else."

Niklaus nodded and followed me. So lost in my train

of thought was I that when I rounded the hallway, I collided with Ashroy, who was exiting his room. He barely moved, but I rocked back on my heels, unsteady, and his hands were quick to right me.

"Good morning to you too." He offered an easy grin, which only grew as Niklaus approached us.

Niklaus, already not in a good mood, glared at Ashroy.

Ashroy chuckled in response. "Both of you are in a mood. A rough night?" His crystal eyes locked with mine.

"I received a letter from Domitia. She demands the return of Niklaus." I shook my head, feeling the tension radiate from my neck to my jaw, and a headache was starting to form.

"No. We have to remain firm in our decision. He stays. She is trying to lure us out, away from our resources." Ashroy sounded exasperated as he looked between us.

"I told her as much." It was like it pained him to agree with Ashroy.

"Let me have at least one cup of tea in me before we rehash the situation," I ground out as I walked away. Not only that, but the others had to be informed too.

"Stasya, wait!" Ashroy called after me.

It took three cups of hot tea and an hour of listening to Ashroy explain how Niklaus remaining in the castle was truly the best option to settle the turmoil inside. And Niklaus agreed. It was the latter that took me by surprise.

Selfishly, I wanted him under the same roof as me. And while I knew this was the smartest action to take, I also wanted this to end as soon as possible. Why couldn't Niklaus snuff her out in the middle of the night?

Ashroy stirred his tea, then sipped it. "I've learned a great deal about her through correspondence with my spymaster, including the patterns of her actions. If it isn't within the scope of her plan, she doesn't do it."

"So, she didn't take into account that we'd imprison an assassin bent on killing me?" I said, exasperated.

Niklaus rolled his eyes. "She didn't account for how quickly a werewolf's body heals. That the Lethe didn't hit me as hard as it would a human."

After breakfast, Niklaus caught my elbow in the hallway, turning me to face him. "This entire thing is more than anyone should have to deal with, but try not to pull away from me. I'm having a difficult time with the flashes of memory and our current predicament." His voice had an edge to it as he pleaded with me. Leaning forward, his lips brushed against my temple. "Be patient."

"I'll try," I said softly.

Niklaus squeezed my elbow where he still held me. He breathed against my temple, then his lips traveled down my cheek, to the corner of my mouth, to my lips. Niklaus' hands cupped my face as he deepened the kiss, drawing it out for as long as he could.

Ashroy cleared his throat, interrupting the intimate moment. He avoided looking in our direction and instead stared at a potted plant. "I thought you'd enjoy this," he began. "I brought a peace offering." Ashroy offered Niklaus a cordial and held one for himself. Lifting his glass, he clinked it against the other. "To sabotage."

Niklaus quirked a red brow and said nothing, but he eyed the contents suspiciously. "What is this?"

Ashroy smiled toothily, his eyes twinkling with mischief. "The reversal," he offered, tilting his head. "If you want it, that is."

My skin broke out into goosebumps at his words. He'd made the elixir?

Niklaus swirled the liquid around in the glass. "I do," he said and nodded. "I want to remember." He lifted it and downed the contents, grimacing as he swallowed.

"Now, we wait," Ashroy offered.

"More waiting. Wonderful." I sighed. "For how long?"

Ashroy shrugged, offering an apologetic look. "I'm uncertain, but I would say within a day."

We would have to work with that.

Ten

I nstead of pacing the halls or running through the same plan we had rehashed several times, I took Niklaus back to my chambers. Alric had relaxed a fraction since the previous night—bless him—and instead of posting guards in the room, he allowed Niklaus and I to be alone.

"Is this what it's going to take to distract you?" Niklaus murmured as the door shut. His eyes searched mine as he walked forward and brushed his knuckles down my cheek. "Tell me what you want, Stasya," he said against my neck, and the roughness of his beard turned my insides to liquid.

It had been too long since we'd first had one another, but it felt wrong asking that of this Niklaus. He didn't remember, didn't know me . . .

"I want you to remember us," I said, grabbing his hand and threading my fingers through his. It was unfair of me to ask, even more unfair to presume he'd want what we had started before.

Niklaus' brow furrowed. "Even after all that I've done?" He glanced down at our hands, and I wondered what was running through his mind. Did he regret dismantling the Council by slaughtering them? His grip loosened, and he hissed as he placed a hand to his head. His knees buckled, and I had to rush forward to keep him from smacking his head on the bedpost.

"Niklaus!" I knelt beside him, grabbing him by the shoulders to prop him against me. "What is wrong?"

He groaned, his head lolling to the side.

"Alric!" I shouted, and a moment later, he rushed in, confusion in his gaze. "Get Ashroy, now!"

"I feel . . . funny," Niklaus slurred. "My arms, I can't move them." His words blended together as he slumped over. "So . . . tired." Then his body went limp.

"Nik!" Panic coursed through me as I shook him again. "Niklaus, wake up!" I touched my fingers to his throat, hoping to feel a pulse. A strong heartbeat bumped against my fingers.

Ashroy ran in and rushed over. "So soon?" he muttered, then helped me get Niklaus into my bed. "Just as Lethe subdues a person, using sleep to strip away memories, so does the reversal. I thought perhaps we'd have until tomorrow, nightfall even, but this . . . could work in our favor, as long as he recovers from his slumber quickly too."

"He was fine until a moment ago. It happened so fast." I sat on the edge of the bed, willing my heart to steady. My fingers coasted along Niklaus' cheek, then into his unruly hair. Even while he slept, his brow was furrowed, and I could nearly picture him smirking.

"Let him rest, Stasya. I increased the dose a fraction to hopefully expedite things, and it seems it worked." He motioned for me to follow him out, and while I wanted to stay and watch over Niklaus, a distraction was welcome.

Before I left, I drew a blanket over Niklaus, then turned away. "Keep guards inside and outside the room. When he wakes, I want to be alerted immediately." Ashroy was several steps ahead of me, and he paused as I quickened my stride to catch up.

"How does the library sound?" He cocked his head, offering a warm smile.

I sighed. "Maybe too quiet for the roaring of my head right now." Honestly, I felt as though I would burst at the seams. Thoughts ran through my head, as did worries. What if Lady Domitia swept in when we least expected it, if Niklaus didn't wake in time, and how would Abendrot recover from all of this?

It seemed no matter how I tried to repair the broken kingdom, it was destined to crumble into ruins.

Ashroy reached out and gripped my shoulder, pulling me into the present. He dipped his head down, catching my lowered gaze. "Hey. You are not alone. And while this is a trying time, I'm here, and so are several others. We will rally around you." He removed his hand but reached for my wrist and gently tugged me along.

Ashroy's arrival seemed to be a distant memory, and

I could have laughed for having thought him to be anything more than what he was: an ally, a friend. I didn't trust that he was exactly what he said because who in this world was ever so honest, so kind?

As soon as he had arrived, I'd wanted to know what Ashroy's stakes in the betrothal were, but it was clear now that he wanted to protect a kingdom from falling like the others, and during his time here, he'd made friends.

Since my father's death, he hadn't pushed the idea of marriage, hadn't even taken me aside to discuss whether it was still an agreement. He'd said he knew I was unavailable, but that didn't mean our betrothal had been severed.

When I entered the library, I smiled at the rows and rows of bookshelves. There were blue spines, red, black, brown, every color imaginable. Ashroy pulled away, heading toward the foreign history section, and I followed closely. He pulled out a book, but I hadn't taken notice of the title.

"I think we need to have a discussion," Ashroy offered.

What was it about those words that could set anyone's heart to racing as if they were in trouble? I turned my attention to the shelf, not feeling the need to grab a history volume. "What is it?"

Ashroy laughed. "You're not in trouble." He motioned toward the table, and together, we walked to it and sat down. He hadn't yet opened the book, and I didn't know if he would because his gaze was locked with mine. "It's about our betrothal."

Oh. He would choose now to discuss it. Chewing on the inside of my lip, I considered what I'd say. "What of it?"

"We haven't had the time to discuss this, but I wanted to clarify something for you." Ashroy turned in his chair to face me. His features remained soft and open. "When your father reached out to Ishkertov, it was with our potential union in mind. To strengthen our ongoing support of one another. And he relayed your truth, knowing that Ishkertov would celebrate what you are rather than shame you."

Father had told me the former, but he hadn't told me that when coming to Abendrot, Ashroy knew my truth. Yes, Ashroy eventually told me, but what was the point of rehashing this now?

"I came here with the intent to come to know you, to see if marriage was what you wanted. Ishkertov doesn't support marriages that aren't agreed on by both parties. It's your choice just as much as it's mine, and . . . I guess my point to this is, what is it that you want?"

My brows furrowed. I wanted my kingdom to be repaired, I wanted us to heal and finally be rid of Domitia and her wicked ways. In order for that to happen, the people needed a strong leader, and while I had been groomed, my father had failed in his last years. I wasn't privy to meetings, I didn't know the innermost workings, and without a Council to guide me . . .

Ashroy was a smart choice. A clear choice.

"Stop," he said and lifted his hand to tuck a finger under my chin. He turned my face toward his and offered a smile. "If you're thinking that hard, then it isn't with your heart. And that is what I want for you: a heart choice, not a kingdom choice."

"But the kingdom needs—"

"A sound ruler, and her happiness comes into play." He dropped his hand to the table. "I know you're capable of ruling, there was never a question about that. In my time here, I've come to adore you, and while there isn't love, I could easily see myself falling for you."

Heat rushed into my cheeks. If I could have crawled beneath a floorboard at the moment, I would have. But this conversation had to happen. "I believe I could love you easily too." And I could. He was genuinely kind, quick-witted, knew more about politics than I likely ever would . . .

"But you cannot?" he prompted.

"Niklaus . . . is my mate, and as ill-matched as we may be, I do love him." Saying it out loud made it real, and it was dizzying. I searched Ashroy's eyes in hopes that I wouldn't detect hurt there, but there was only his gentle smile.

"I know. And, despite Niklaus being . . . Niklaus, I think he loves you too. I have no doubt that he would tear the entire forest down and raze villages if it meant protecting you." He chuckled at this. "And maybe just for fun too." Ashroy grimaced at that.

Tears sprang to my eyes, all the emotions from the past few days catching up to me. I was grateful for how understanding Ashroy was and that, through the mayhem that had ensued since his arrival, he was still able to assess the situation and help me.

"I suppose that means you'll have to leave when this is all done," I said softly and reached for his hand, squeezing it. "I have truly cherished our time together, Ashroy, and I am so sorry you've had to endure more than you bargained for."

He lowered his eyes and chuckled. "I don't think anyone could have foreseen that, and while it was terrible, I strive to see a positive in the situation. I have a better understanding of your wolf boy, and I'd also like to think it brought you and I closer too." Ashroy sighed and shook his head. "My father implored me to return, that he would send troops no matter what but that my safety came first." He leaned back in his chair, then shot me a look. "I will not abandon you during your time of need. I'd be a piss-poor excuse of an ally, let alone a friend. Besides that, the last I heard, your coronation was in three months."

A small, hysterical laugh shook my shoulders again. "If there is even—"

Ashroy squinted at me, covering my lips with his finger. "There will be. I'm not letting you ditch your role here, and I know several others who feel the same. Your people need you more than ever, and they sing your praises for what you've accomplished in such a short amount of time." He dropped his hand to his side. "When things are set to rights, that is when I'll leave, but not a moment sooner."

If circumstances had been different, I could have seen myself falling in love with Ashroy and spending the rest of my days with him. His beauty was as harsh as the land he came from, but in his gaze were intelligence and sincerity. Ashroy was there when I needed him, endured far more than he should have, and he protected us the best he could. However, the only affection I felt toward him was the same I felt toward Edda. It wasn't lost on me that my life would have been a great deal easier if only I'd chosen Ashroy, but that wasn't what my heart yearned for.

"Thank you—for everything. I don't know what I would have done if you weren't here." That was the truth. Ashroy had been a voice of reason amongst the madness, and when I was floundering, he'd offered his hand to help me out of the unknown waters that threatened to drown me.

I leaned forward, throwing my arms around his neck. His arms encircled me as I held him tightly. Turning my head, I brushed a kiss to his temple. "Thank you," I said again.

He smoothed the hair against my back and laughed softly. "You would have done exactly as you are. Don't you see what you have accomplished without me? You reached out to alliances, strengthened them and the core of your country. I think you should give yourself some credit, Stasya."

"I'm sorry for the times I was out of line. You didn't deserve an attitude." Guilt clawed into my heart as if it were made of paper. There were several times I'd lashed out, and each time, he had graciously offered amiable words. He had only stormed off once, and I was in the wrong. I didn't deserve his kindness.

"I'm from Ishkertov, where the women are as brutal as the winters. If I didn't manage to grow thick skin in my youth, I'd never have made it to adulthood." Ashroy chuckled, withdrawing from me. "I'm not a dullard. I know that your anger comes from a place of hurt, uncertainty, and fear. All I ask is that you *try* to trust me."

I nodded my agreement, knowing that if I opted to speak, I'd just end up mumbling through tears. The claws that had been shredding the paper-thin contents of my heart finished the job, and my chest constricted as guilt flooded my entire being.

"And there is one thing I've forgotten to mention . . . Among the letters I sent with Niklaus, I had penned some for Domitia's troops. Niklaus doesn't know this because I figured if he was pressed, or if he decided to side with Domitia . . ." His gaze flicked to the side, and his lips twitched.

My eyes widened, and I stared at him, unsure if I should be mad or glad. "Let's hope it pays off."

A throat cleared behind us, disrupting the moment. "Your Highness, pardon the interruption, but I thought perhaps my princess would benefit from sword practice." It was Alric. I didn't have to turn around to know that he wore his stoic expression or that his dark gaze was fixated on me.

"Well, do you think you'd enjoy that?" Ashroy asked me.

"I think I would." I pulled away from him, pausing mid-turn. "Ashroy, thank you. I cherish our friendship more than you know."

He nodded, smiling. "Thank you for that."

I walked toward Alric, who lifted a brow in question. He didn't say a word, not until we were in the hallway.

"I'm glad I didn't have to pull you off him."

Silence stretched between us, and my cheeks reddened with shame. Had Alric heard all of that? "You were . . . listening?"

"I blocked out the mushy parts." He grinned, and while I wanted nothing more than to berate him for listening, it *was* his job to shadow me. Besides that, his grin was childlike, and I couldn't help but laugh.

Eleven

S weat trickled down my neck from sparring with Alric. Every muscle burned, but it was good, and I felt more alive than I had recently. I needed a bath, and then I'd check on Niklaus—

Frederik rushed into the courtyard, eyes gleaming a brilliant green. "They're all dead." His gaze locked onto mine. "They're dead," he echoed, this time with a smile curling his lips.

I stepped forward and placed my hand against Frederik's forearm. "Who, Freddy?"

Fear uncurled, snaking around my insides.

He swallowed, nodding his head. "The lady's team. We took them out early this morning." Frederik's words were clear, but they were clipped and left much to the imagination.

"Lady Domitia's team?" I mused out loud. My body

instantly stiffened. I thought we'd have a few days or weeks, not a day. "Where is Sabrina?"

Frederik's full bottom lip stuck out, and he lifted a hand to scrape at the side of his face. "Lukas was hurt, so she took him back to headquarters since it was closer."

I cursed none too quietly. "Can you take me to the headquarters? I need to see Sabrina and make sure Lukas is okay." When Frederik turned away, he exuded uncertainty in waves. "Damn their rules, Frederik. I am soon to be the queen, and as such, I demand you show me the way."

My words must have rattled him because he nodded and rushed down the hall, toward the exit of the castle. Much to my relief, no one stopped us, and no one questioned where I was going.

When I reached the forest, that's when I heard him—Alric, shouting my name in a desperate attempt to call me back. Frederik turned his back to me, allowing me privacy, and I stripped down to bare skin.

"Show me the way, Frederik." We shifted then, and as my guide bolted into the woods, so did I.

Briars, branches, and underbrush snagged at my pelt, tearing tufts of white fur away. Frederik kept a relentless pace, diving over fallen trees and dipping under low-hanging limbs. He was used to running, and sadly, I wasn't. When I inevitably fell behind, he'd slow and wait for me until I caught back up. We ran for a half hour until we arrived at the Huntsmen's headquarters.

I had no clothes with me, but as I shifted, I moved my hair to fall over my breasts. Frederik didn't shift back. Instead, he moved in front of me, acting as a shield.

"Thank you," I panted, feeling my heart thundering away wildly. My breath came in uneven heaves from the sprint through the woods.

We walked inside the oversized cottage; the front hall was empty. A coat hung on a rack, and I wrapped it around myself before padding over to a nearby room. I could hear raspy breaths coming from behind the door.

"Sabrina?" I called out and opened the door.

I gasped, nearly choking at the sight of Lukas sprawled on a table, gripping the sides of it as Sabrina cleansed a deep gash on his stomach.

Sabrina didn't so much as lift her gaze from the wound. "Frederik led you here, I see." Her voice was shaky as she stitched the wound together. "It seems someone forgot the rules." She snipped the thread once she finished closing the gash. Sabrina's eyes didn't waver from her twin, and her bloodied hand ran against his cheek. "You will be okay."

"We'll see," Lukas said through gritted teeth. He grunted, allowing himself to lay out flat.

"What happened? Frederik said . . . they're all dead?" I moved out of the way as Sabrina walked toward the washbasin beside me. "What happened?"

Sabrina's expression tightened. Her lips pressed into a thin line, and it wasn't lost on me that her brow twitched. "We were ambushed, but we had Raif and Frederik waiting in the wings. They weren't anticipating the wolves slaughtering them, but they attacked us first and without mercy. They fought like they were possessed, and with little finesse, might I add." Sabrina shook her hands out and dried them on a towel. "Lukas was stabbed with a laced dagger. I think I got everything out in time, and I gave him an elixir for the poison."

I walked up to where Lukas lay sprawled, his blue eyes closed as he rested. The sound of his ragged breaths touched my ears. The sight of him laid out on the bed brought back the memory of my father dying, and I couldn't keep my tears at bay.

"I'll kill her for this. For everything she has done. I swear to you, I will kill her." I leaned forward and kissed Lukas' sweaty brow. I'd accepted him as a part of my new family, like a cousin or older brother. He was always kind to me, and honest.

Sabrina smiled faintly. "I pried information from one assailant. He was reluctant, but I can be fairly persuasive when I want to be." She chuckled darkly and continued. "One of her men said she's coming for you, but that wasn't good enough for me. I wanted to know exactly when she planned on doing it. If he knew, he'd spill it."

I didn't want to know how she extracted the information from the man, but my imagination filled in the gaps. "Did he end up talking?"

"Talking . . . screaming. They're the same, aren't they?" She paused in between speaking, making me long to shake her for the rest of the story. "He bled the information along with his life force. The Hawk—Domitia—

plans to arrive before dawn, and that is as much as he knew." Sabrina cocked her hip as she leaned against the table, her shrewd eyes never leaving me. "Raif was carrying this message to the castle, so when you return, I assume the entire castle will be abuzz." Sabrina rubbed her face. Exhaustion exuded from her, but her eyes were still as bright and focused as ever. "I hope you're ready, because whether you are or not, the Hawk is on her way."

"Niklaus is in a deep sleep." I combed my fingers through my hair, loosing a tense breath. "Ashroy gave him the cure to his lost memories. But he hasn't awakened yet. I don't know when he will. Ashroy said within a day—"

"You don't need Niklaus. He is a good asset to have, but your army is primed and ready. All of you are. Let her come to you in desperation. Let her try to get to you. She will fail." Sabrina nodded her head and glanced down at her brother. "I hope whoever deals the killing blow draws it out."

Frederik nosed his way into the room, still in wolf form. I turned on my heel and welcomed him to my side. He pressed his auburn head against me, and I stroked his soft, tufted ear. "I'm ready for this to be over, because I know something that Domitia doesn't."

Sabrina leaned over and grabbed her brother's hand, stroking it with her other. "I have no doubt that Niklaus will wake in his own time." She glanced up at me. "Lukas will have to sit this one out, but I'll be there. You can count on that."

I nodded and turned on my heel. "I suggest riding as fast as you can as soon as you can."

We would be ready, but for now, I needed to get back to the castle before it was too late.

WE KEPT a punishing pace on the return to the castle. If I'd thought it was quick before, it was even faster now. I could smell the trail we left on our way to headquarters, and so I didn't rely on Frederik to lead the way. I dove around him, weaving in and out of the brush. My limbs were tired of being pushed, tired from the previous exertion of running, and my lungs felt as though they would burst.

When the castle came into view, I slowed. My body shifted back quickly, and I dragged my clothes back on, not caring that I was barefoot in the snow.

"Frederik, get dressed and follow me!" I called out, panting hard. I ran toward the castle gates, and frantic faces met mine.

"Princess?" a guard inquired.

I nodded my head as the iron gate swung open. Frederik ran behind me as I ran up the stairs and entered the castle. Sabrina was right, as I'd known she would be. The castle hummed with anxiety, but it was Alric who approached me first and grabbed my shoulders.

"Where have you been?" he demanded.

The air couldn't flood my lungs fast enough as I panted from the exertion. "Sabrina . . ." I rubbed my chest and glanced around, looking for Raif. "Raif?" I questioned, waiting for Alric to confirm or press for more information.

"He told us. Gods above, Stasya." His fingers bit into my shoulders with more force, and he must have realized that because he pulled his hands away, then put them on his hips. "Your sister has been a wreck." Alric knew where to hit me with a low blow, that was for certain.

I spread my arms wide and glared at him. "Here I am! I am well and alive for gods only know how long. Raif brought the message, I assume?" Each word ended with a gasp. Breathing was a touch easier now as my heart slowed to a normal pace.

Alric bowed his head. "Forgive me, Majesty. I worried about your wellbeing." Even with his head lowered and tone quiet, I could hear the underlying bite to his words. I'd deal with that later.

I clenched my jaw but didn't retort. "Niklaus . . . he hasn't awakened yet?" Alric shook his head and I sighed. "Is everyone preparing? Where is Edda?" It wasn't lost on me what I must look like. Hair unbound, wild, and potentially housing a few leaves. My feet were bare, bright red from trekking through the snow, and my cheeks were rosy from a combination of the chilly air and running.

"We are readying." Alric followed on my heels as I

wound through the hall toward the heart of the castle. "She is in the library with Prince Ashroy."

I nodded. Edda would be fine in his company. There was something about him that soothed her, and I imagined it was that he had been there in the darkest hour. However, I knew my sister, and if she didn't see me the moment I stepped foot in the castle again, she'd storm into my room like a cyclone and berate me.

The inhabitants of the castle may have been frenzied by their anxiety, but it was quiet enough that every time one of my feet struck the floor, it echoed in the hall. Quickening my stride, I made it to the library and sighed at the sight of my sister. She was safe and unharmed. Ashroy sat at the table with her, chatting softly. The massive windows in the room shed the late afternoon's sunlight on the table, bathing my sister and Ashroy in a golden halo.

"How fitting that the two troublemakers are together." I smiled, laughing as my sister flung herself from her chair and flew into my arms. "I'm okay, Edda. This will all end soon." No matter what the outcome, it would end come dawn, and I was more than ready for that. "For now, we plan and get a little rest."

"Honestly, you need to be more careful." Edda shook her head, stepping backward.

It wasn't lost on me how my younger sister was chastising me for being reckless or that she took on the mothering tone I had frequently used on her. Sighing, I lifted my hand and tapped the tip of her nose.

"I'm not sure what to call you now. Edda the Lion or Edda the Wise?" I teased lightly.

"The Wise Lion has a ring to it," she retorted, grinning broadly.

Ashroy spoke from the table, smirking. "Likely the most accurate, if you ask me." He caught my gaze and lifted his eyebrows, a question swirling within his eyes.

I ignored the look and continued on. "After I wash up, we'll be holding a meeting. I'll see you there."

Without another word, I left to do just as I said. I direly needed a bath, and I hoped the warmth would settle my growing nerves. But the more time ticked on, the more unease nipped at my core and unsettled me. As much as I wanted to check on Niklaus myself, I had other matters to attend to.

Whatever happened tomorrow would most assuredly change everything.

THE MOON TOOK its sister's place in the sky and hung brightly against the velveteen blanket of night. Stars contrasted with the dark canvas, twinkling with their silent chatter. We'd been sitting in the room for two hours already, and it must have been midnight or later.

Alric groaned from where he sat at the meeting table, his hands raking through his hair. More than once, he'd implored me to remain safe and away from the heat of the battle, but I refused. What message would that send to my citizens, and what example would I be setting for my sister if I ran with my tail between my legs? I knew the dangers. I also knew that it was my stubborn streak that told me to stand my ground and fight.

"And what happens if you fall?" Alric asked softly.

My fingers gripped the back of the oak chair. "Then Edda takes my place in the line of succession. Because I will be amidst the battle, my sister isn't to leave a safe room. That is an order, please go see to that."

Alric nodded and reluctantly left the room.

This time, during the meeting, the general of Abendrot's army sat in. His shrewd gaze cut across the table and found mine. "Your forces are in place, in the forest lying in wait, and also in the courtyard. Since we're not certain how many are coming to her aid, it's best we have more than we think we need."

I nodded. "I think so too."

"I can't say for certain how many, but I know it isn't what she thinks she has," Ashroy added.

Raif pushed away from the wall, the shadows almost swallowing him whole. His green eyes filled with concern as he signed slowly so that I could make out each word. "Are you sure about all of this?"

Thanks to Elka's teachings, I could muddle my way through interpreting signing. My shoulders slumped. "As sure as we can be. The only thing I am sure of is that I will be the one to deal the killing blow to Domitia."

"I'll be there by your side, just in case you miss,"

Sabrina said with a wicked grin. As promised, she had arrived not long after I had.

And if she killed me first, so be it. But the satisfaction of ending Domitia's life belonged to me. No one would steal that moment away; I forbade it.

Raif grinned from ear to ear, flashing his pearly whites. "We will save that pleasure for you, my princess." He bowed low at the waist, and when he stood upright, he winked.

"We should all get ready now," I said, but my voice sounded strange and distant to my ears.

Raif nodded and left the room.

With Niklaus still in a deep slumber, I left for the armory to prepare. He needed to rest, needed to recover from the effects of the elixir. I only hoped that he remained asleep for it all, and if I should fall, that he not wake until it was all over.

Inside the armory, servants awaited my arrival and started to prepare the undergarments and lightweight leathers. I stripped, and then piece by piece, I was clad in protective gear. When they were finished, a group of guards escorted me into the courtyard.

I remained with the guards, who hovered closely. Alric was among them, to my left.

"It isn't too late to return inside," he groused.

I glanced at the sky and judged the position of the moon. If Sabrina was right, it would be at least two hours more. But if I had learned anything of Domitia, it was that she would come earlier to throw us off. Only time would tell.

Whatever time we thought we had, we didn't.

It was an hour into our wait when a torch flew into the air, followed by the warning cry of an approaching party.

The roar of soldiers went up in the air, and then the courtyard became a frenzy of activity, though the guards around me kept their positions.

"Draw your sword, Your Highness," Alric prompted, and I did. "And whatever you do, stay with us."

The next few moments were a flurry of movement I couldn't fully keep track of. One moment, I was standing with my guards; the next, the soldiers converged on the iron gates, and while they remained locked, they bowed from the outside pressure of the troops Domitia had brought.

Everyone's attention was focused on the gate, but from the corner of my eye, I saw someone scale the wall, climb down, and race directly toward me.

"Shit, Alric!" I screamed the moment Domitia let loose a bolt from her crossbow. The guard to my right didn't have enough time to raise his shield, and so he leaped in front of the arrow, and it pierced his throat, spraying blood in my face

"It is over, Domitia." I stepped around my guards, sword in hand. "You have no army. What alliances you thought you had have now crept back into the holes they came from, and those who refused are now rotting corpses. If you and your small forces continue, that's all you'll be too."

I was close enough to the gate that I could see doubt

flicker in the depths of Domitia's eyes. Perhaps it was the fact that I used her real name—or it could have been the mention of her alliances. None of it mattered. She was desperate and would no doubt fight until the end. Until one of us drew our last breath.

"I don't believe you," she hissed.

Twelve

I woke with a start. My head throbbed violently, and the urge to vomit propelled me from bed. Stumbling, I collapsed to the cool floor and spewed into the corner until the dizziness passed.

Wiping the spittle from my mouth, I rose and swayed as I glanced around the room. Stasya. Where was she? I winced, a flicker of a memory breaking through.

Stasya's hair, covered in black. The look of happiness shimmering in her gaze as we ventured into the forest together . . .

Stasya.

I blinked and focused on my breathing until my heart rate returned to normal. I didn't get much time because just then, cries rang out. Racing to the window, I peered down. Although there wasn't a courtyard view, I could see torches in the woods.

Memories of now and months ago collided, not making sense. But I knew one thing: the Hawk—Lady Domitia—must have been knocking.

Where was Stasya?

She better not have gone outside—I knew better than that, so why even bother? What good was I now, unsure on my feet, head throbbing?

Shaking my head, I snorted. "Better than most." Muttering, I left the room, and once the floor didn't feel as though it was tipping, I ran down the hall and through the doors.

Domitia jerked her head in my direction, her lips twisting as she took notice of me. The glint in her eye said she believed I still didn't remember a damn thing.

"My dear hunter," she drawled. "Have they been keeping you penned? I told you they were wicked." Domitia stepped backward as the guards surrounding Stasya pushed forward, while shoving her away from the threat of Domitia.

Stasya's eyes were on me, as if she didn't believe I was there—or awake. Her gaze flicked away as she realized what her guards were doing.

"They stripped me of my weapons," I said, which wasn't a lie, and crossed the distance between us. Domitia reached for her back, where a hilt jutted out, and pulled the sword free, handing it over. It was stupid and trusting on her part, but I'd play a game with her if that was what she wanted.

Domitia waved me on. "Now, hunter." She stood

back like a cowardly handler as she sent me off to fight for her.

"As my lady commands, so it shall be." With both my hands on the hilt of the blade, I lunged for one of Stasya's guards. Meeting his gaze, I lifted my eyebrows and winked. He was one that had guarded me in Stasya's room, and I hoped to heavens he realized what I was about to do. Thrusting the sword forward, I aimed between his arm and ribs, sliding into a sweet spot without gutting him.

Dammit all. I was still so bloody dizzy, just rushing forward almost sent me to my knees. I had to keep moving, had to keep breathing through the light-headedness.

The guard fell, and I advanced on the next one. My knee rose, colliding to make him double over. "I'm not going to hurt you," I ground out loud enough for him to hear, and he fell away, scrambling to get up. I had to give them credit; they were superb actors.

The others didn't stand around waiting for their turn. Instead, they advanced on Domitia. I turned on my heel, wondering where Stasya had gone. She and Alric had crept backward as the fight raged on, but where had she gone to?

Thirteen

"Open the gate," I ordered.

"Are you mad?" Alric snapped.

"Let them come inside, and we will see who will reign over this kingdom. They're outnumbered, Alric!"

Reluctantly, Alric cried out the order, and the guards obeyed, then joined their comrades behind them.

Niklaus' eyes were cold and devoid of emotion. Fear sliced through me, and I wondered if the elixir Ashròy had given him had done its job. Or if it would take longer than a day. We didn't *have* that long!

The moment the gate opened, droves of assailants flooded through, and that was all the prompting I needed to move the sword upward as more individuals ran toward me.

"Shit, Stasya, we need to get you in an assembly of guards again," Alric shouted over the melee. He blocked an assailant with his sword, smacking it away before embedding it into his side. From the corner of my eye, I recognized Sabrina. She danced around her victims, cutting, slicing, and stabbing them with her twin swords. Even though Alric had spent hours upon hours training me to wield a blade, I knew I wasn't a sword master. I'd grown stronger, faster, and learned how to read my opponent's intent, but I wasn't a warrior. Now, I had no choice but to be.

Despite Alric's wishes, he was pushed farther away as two individuals cut him off from me. And at the same time, a tall woman charged at me full speed, two long daggers in each hand. She swept one blade low, which I blocked, but her other one caught my sword and tipped it downward. If she were stronger than me, it would have kept my weapon lowered, but I had the advantage of being a wolf, and I flicked her arms upward with a push. Just as I was advancing on her, driving her backward, there was a blur of movement behind her, and then a gleam of metal jutted from the woman's chest.

I gasped as blood sprayed from the gaping hole. The woman fell to the ground, revealing Niklaus standing behind her. He yanked the sword free before stalking off to find another victim. If I'd had any doubts as to whose side he was on, Niklaus had just confirmed then that he was on ours.

I took a moment to gather my wits, to look around, and I saw Domitia cutting down one of my guards. She was oblivious to her hunter's betrayal. Fury surged through me as the guard collapsed to the ground, fueling my limbs with the need to press on.

One by one, Domitia's followers fell. Skilled or not, she had arrived outnumbered. Any my guards and I didn't take down, Niklaus did.

Every muscle in my body screamed as I fought alongside Alric, dancing in a circle with our opponents. From the corner of my eye, I saw a sword penetrate Alric's side, and he doubled over, trying to fend off his attacker. I screamed, lunging forward to jump at my assailant, and the tip of my sword slid through his neck, silencing his shouting.

Alric lifted his sword just in time to fend off the blade moving in for a lethal blow. I spun around and drove them backward, allowing Alric to recover.

"Get back, Alric." Lowering my body, I dipped low and swiped at the attacker, pressing him back into the throng of my guards.

"Stasya!" Alric bellowed.

Something pinched my side, and as I turned to face it, I realized it was a dagger, still held by Domitia. She twisted it, then pulled it out to hold it against my throat in a desperate move.

"Drop your sword and call them off," she ordered.

The dagger's pressure increased, biting into the tender flesh. I dropped the sword but refused to call my men off. "No. You're out of moves, and you will die by sunrise."

She twisted her hand in my braid, yanking it so my head twisted to the side.

"Don't make me laugh." Her fingers tightened in my hair all the more, eliciting a cry of pain from me.

Niklaus ceased fighting. His sword hung low to his side as he approached us. His yellow eyes regarded me with an unreadable expression, then he looked to Domitia expectantly.

"Kill her, hunter! Kill her now!" Domitia shrieked. Niklaus hesitated, and that was all she needed. "You . . ." The realization must have dawned on her as she scowled at him. "No matter, I'll do it myself."

She lifted the blade from my neck in a fluid motion, raised it above her head, and would have impaled my heart with it—had her arm remained intact.

A snarl tore free from a wolf behind us. I wasn't sure who it was. But one moment, Domitia's arm lifted, and the next, it was gone. Cries of pain filled the air as she stumbled backward. I saw the window of opportunity and clambered for the sword I had discarded moments ago. Once it was in my hands, I ran forward, shoving it deep into her chest with every ounce of hatred I held.

"Long live the queen," I growled in her face, then watched as she fell to the ground.

Domitia's hair covered her bloodied face, once beautiful and now marred with pain. She sputtered, gasping for breath as blood filled her mouth. In the next shuddering breath, she drew her last gulp of air before dying.

A red wolf bared his teeth at the fallen woman, the same wolf that had torn her arm off, then closed the distance between us. His head bumped against mine, and I shakily exhaled.

"Thank you, Frederik. It's over."

"Stasya!" Niklaus barreled his way toward me, noting

the bleeding gash at my side and the blood dripping down my throat.

He dropped the sword in his grasp, lifted his hands, and cupped my face. "I thought she was going to . . ." He exhaled raggedly before continuing. "I thought you were dead, and I've never been that terrified in my life." Niklaus swallowed; his tone was rough. "I couldn't live with myself if that happened."

I closed my eyes, absorbing his words. This was my Niklaus, the one I'd grown to love. "It's over," I mumbled, choking on a sob. My hand moved to the throbbing pain in my abdomen, and soon, it was coated in warm blood. Perhaps I was in shock. I wasn't comprehending the moment. "Where is Alric?"

"He's being tended to. Let's do the same for you."

Niklaus pulled back, glancing down at my wound. With care, he lifted me into his arms and strode toward the castle. Whether from exhaustion or the loss of blood, when I closed my eyes, I fell into the welcoming darkness.

The next time my eyes opened, Edda was staring down at me, her curls framing her cherubic face. "You're awake. Ashroy, Niklaus, she's awake!" Edda raised her voice as she looked over her shoulder.

Although the light was dim in my room, it still blinded me. I squinted, just barely able to make out the two figures in chairs next to my bed. They quickly stood up and shuffled over to the bed.

Edda brushed her fingers along my forehead, smiling. "You lost a lot of blood, and that dagger was poisoned. Ashroy was able to heal you."

Ashroy? I blinked away the grogginess, gingerly sitting up. "He couldn't have," I whispered.

The memory of the dagger piercing my abdomen brought forth a shudder, but when I reached under the blankets and felt my stomach, there was nothing but a raised scar.

"On the contrary, my dear, I did. You killed Domitia, so it broke the enchantment." Ashroy reached for my other hand, grabbed it, and squeezed.

The bed dipped down as Niklaus crawled onto it, then found his place next to me. Dipping his head, he brushed a tender kiss to my forehead and said, "Next time, hide with Ashroy and Edda." He chuckled as Ashroy clucked his tongue in response.

Ashroy huffed. "I wasn't hiding. I was making sure Edda didn't follow in her sister's footsteps and do something foolish."

Edda grumbled, which was her way of agreeing with the one she was arguing with.

I laughed, regretting the act immediately. The muscles in my side throbbed, and I wasn't sure if it was from the exertion of the fight or the healed wound. "What time is it?"

"Late noon. Two days after the battle, mind you." It was Alric's voice, and I nearly leaped from the bed. Niklaus' hand steadied me where I lay, and the honorable captain moved forward.

"Well, well, if it isn't the wolf queen."

Tears streamed down my face as he approached my beside. Ashroy stepped aside and allowed Alric to step in, and he lowered himself so I could hug him.

"I thought you . . ."

"You're not the only stubborn one, and if it weren't for Ashroy, I think I would be dead." Alric looked to Ashroy and gave him an appreciative nod. "Anyway, I wanted to see with my own eyes that you were well again. It looks like our practice paid off after all."

His words immediately made me laugh, but it was true. The time spent with Alric learning how to properly wield a sword and anticipate an opponent's moves proved to be lifesaving.

One after another, visitors came into the room—Frederik, Raif, Sabrina, and Lukas. By the time the last visitor exited, I was exhausted again. Niklaus hadn't left during the visitations, and when he saw my eyelids beginning to droop, he pulled me against his chest.

"Sleep. Tomorrow is another day, and everyone can wait for you." Niklaus dragged his fingers through my hair, enticing goosebumps to form.

I nuzzled against his chest, listening to the steady thrum of it. A question tickled the back of my mind, and as much as I yearned for sleep, I asked it anyway. "Do you remember when you were here before . . . before you forgot me?"

Silence stretched between us. Niklaus dragged his fingers down the back of my neck, and he chuckled. "You mean when you had me at your mercy? Bound and kneeling on the floor? Mm, how could I forget?" He grinned, sliding his hand beneath my chin so he could tilt my head backward. "You're difficult to forget, Stasya. It would take a lot more than poison to make me forget you." Niklaus dipped his head, pressing his lips to mine in a tender, slow kiss. "And to think . . . you did this all for me," he mumbled against my lips, drawing the kiss out.

"Gods, I love you, you infuriating male." What did it matter if I did it for him or the country? I would not argue with him for once, and the fact that my words easily slipped from my lips stunned the pair of us.

"Say it again," Niklaus demanded gently. His gaze held mine as he awaited the words.

"I love you," I repeated. He smiled crookedly in response, but before he could speak again, I interjected. "And I have a proposition for you."

Niklaus' eyebrow quirked in question. "Please, do continue."

I lifted a hand, trying to calm my galloping heart, but what was about to come out of my mouth threatened to steal my breath away. "Will . . . will you stay with me?"

Perhaps it was a premature question, but we already belonged to each other in a deeper, more permanent way. This would be for the country; this would be so all could see that we belonged to one another.

The sound of my heart pounding in my ears deafened me. Since I'd had the dream weeks ago, I couldn't put the notion of marriage from my mind. In the dream, it had seemed far easier.

Niklaus responded with a deep, raspy laugh. "*The*

Royal Consort, it has a ring to it." He lowered his head to place a kiss at my pulse, which did nothing but quicken it. "Yes, I will."

Relief flooded me, allowing my body to sag into his. "One more thing . . ."

Niklaus sighed heavily, almost growling, but it was done in play. "What is it now, woman?" He pulled his head back until we were nose to nose.

"Bring me home to your family. They must be worried sick about you, and I want to meet them on good terms."

Niklaus' nose wrinkled, but he nodded in agreement. "When you've rested, we will visit them. Now, close your eyes before I have Ashroy conjure up a sleeping draught and drug you myself."

"You wouldn't."

"Don't tempt me." Niklaus tugged the blankets up to my chin and winked. "Sleep now, I'll stay with you."

"As you wish."

I closed my eyes, allowing the scent of pine mixed with a smoky musk that was all him to fill my senses. His fingers stroked against my shoulder in a rhythmic motion that had me falling into darkness.

Fourteen

When I was well enough to sit and travel, Niklaus and I journeyed to his home for an early supper. My heart raced wildly and I wiped my clammy hands on my dress more than once. I'd met his sister under different circumstances, but I'd never met his stepfather, Lu, or his mother. To say I was on edge would be an understatement.

"You've already met Liesel, why are you so nervous?" Niklaus chuckled as he opened the carriage door.

After the attack, Niklaus had returned home to reassure them he was, in fact, alive. He'd relayed as many facts as he could without divulging the whole truth.

"This is different. What if your mother doesn't like me?"

Niklaus laughed and reached for my hand. "Stasya, my mother is perhaps one of the most gracious individuals that I know. She will *love* you." He leaned closer. His lips grazed my ear, and then, "Just like *I* love you."

His words stilled me. Niklaus had never said it, but he'd acted on it. Protected me, caressed my body, and when I thought I'd lost him for good, he had returned. So I knew he felt something, but hearing the words tumble from his lips . . .

I turned to look at him, and for once, his eyes lacked their hardness, and there was a gentle, *warm* quality shimmering in their depths.

"I love you too."

Niklaus opened the door to the carriage and hopped out, then held his hand out to me. I stepped down, eyeing the quaint home that had shaped him into who he was.

The air smelled of crisp winter; the scent of burning pine hung in the air, as did the smoke from the nearby chimneys. Despite the business of the village, the freshly fallen snow muted the hustle and bustle of the villagers. There was also the scent of baked pies wafting around as the breeze picked up, and the smell reminded me I was hungry.

Niklaus walked me to the door, opened it without preamble, and shouted, "Anyone home?" He waited a moment, then shouted, "Liesel!"

The way he said her name had me shaking with laughter. I'd never heard someone throw in a half yodel with someone's name before, but Niklaus had done just that. "All right. We're leaving!" He pulled me into their home quickly, slamming the door as if he'd just left.

"Oh no you don't!" a voice shouted, and someone barreled around the corner. Liesel stood with her hands on her hips and her bottom lip jutting out. "Get your behind back here, Niklaus!"

She stormed up to him, apparently oblivious to my presence, and began yanking him deeper into the house. He laughed at her antics, as if this was a normal occurrence, and followed her.

I followed them into the kitchen and saw a table fit for a banquet, and I smiled, touching my chest. "This is wonderful."

Liesel's eyes, so much like her brother's, found mine, and she grinned. "I was busy—well, *we* were busy." She motioned to Lu, then her mother. "So, I hope you're hungry."

Heidi's cheeks flushed and she bobbed a curtsy. "It is an honor, Your Highness." She glanced at Niklaus, then back at me.

Lu slid his arm around Heidi's waist. It was hard to picture the small female with Gregor. I'd known him all my life, and he had been nothing but unpleasant. How she'd ever ended up with him, or how the bond called those two together, I'd never understand. Although, considering my mate, I wondered if there was ever a rhyme or reason to it?

"I'm honored to be here and meet Niklaus' family. He talks about you all the time, and I hear this is where the best roast pig comes from. And pies too."

Liesel grinned. "It's true."

Heidi motioned to the small wooden table. "Please, sit."

So I did, and before we picked up our forks to eat, I wanted to begin on the right foot. "I know Niklaus kept you apprised of the situation," I said, glancing over at him. His brow twitched as he gulped down cider. "But I don't know if I trust that he's told you everything."

"What do you mean?" Heidi pressed. "Niki?"

Niklaus shot me another look as if to say "thanks a lot."

"I suppose you could say, you'll be invited to the castle more often for family dinners." I offered a small smile to Heidi, and as understanding registered, she gasped and stood.

"Is this true? Did you—"

Niklaus leaned back and nodded. A rare, genuine smile touched his lips. "I did."

"Oh, Niki! S—Your Highness—" Heidi fumbled with what to call me given the new situation, and I laughed.

"Please, call me Stasya."

"I knew one day you'd hear the call, Niklaus, but never . . . Heavens." Heidi fanned herself and laughed. "Forgive me."

After we had all eaten our fill, the excitement still filled the small space, but it warmed me to the core and brought me happiness I hadn't felt in a long time, if ever.

Liesel sipped at her flagon of cider. "I still don't believe it. A princess, Niklaus?"

"Technically, queen," Niklaus teased.

Lu sat back, folding his arms over his chest. "You

know . . . I don't think your mother ever told you about the story of when she was a girl in Bromiel," he said, shooting his wife a glance.

Niklaus had told me once that Heidi relished the art of telling stories. So, when she cleared her throat, we all turned to listen. "When I was a girl in Bromiel, the then King Aslaug and Prince Ansgar were to visit and discuss trade options." She waved her hand, smiling. "An arrow impaled the king during the tour, narrowly missing his artery, and it was up to me to save him."

Heidi stopped the story there and picked at the blueberry pie in front of her.

"Oh, come on!" Niklaus said, exasperated. "You can't stop there."

"Now, just a minute." Heidi swallowed her bite of pie and lifted her eyebrows. "I saved the king then and there, even though the prince was less than pleased about it. King Aslaug lived, and the rest you all know. I thought you'd find it amusing to know that on that one day in history, your families were united. Now, they'll be united a little more permanently."

That sounded about right. I imagined my father, brows drawn and lips twisted in a small scowl, as he surveyed the less-than-ideal conditions. I laughed, swiping at a tear beneath my eye. "I never knew this story."

It wasn't as if my father would have boasted about it, but it made sense as to why he refused to step into Bromiel. I realized that my decision to help Bromiel had righted a wrong my father committed a long time ago.

"Thank you for sharing that story, Heidi."

After supper, Niklaus brought me outside to a wooden swing that still hung from a massive tree. He sat down first, then pulled me onto his lap.

"It's curious how things work out, isn't it?" I asked him.

He buried his nose in my braid, toying with the very end of it. "Mm . . . I guess." Niklaus lifted his head and caught my sideward glance. "If you ask me, nothing worked out, Stasya, we fought for it. In life, the things you wish for—the things you need—you fight for them."

Niklaus' words caught me off guard, then I spun sideways on his lap and wrapped an arm around his shoulder. "Would you fight for it all over again?"

He lowered his light red lashes, a crooked grin tilting his lips. "Every inch of the way."

I wasn't sure if we were talking about the same thing, and I suppose it didn't matter. We both fought every inch of the way. We fought against falling in love, and we fought for those we loved.

"I love you," I murmured, leaning in to kiss him.

"I know," he replied. "I love you too."

The Big Bad Wolf belonged to me, and I belonged to him.

WHEN THE SUN grew stronger and blossoms formed on the trees, that's when I knew the coronation was around the corner. The castle teemed with life as everyone prepared for the monumental day, hanging decorations and filling vases with fragrant flowers. It was a relief to see life breathed back into my home.

"I hope you don't get any ideas now," Niklaus said by my ear, tickling the tender flesh.

I shivered, pulling my gloves on. "About what, exactly?"

"Thinking you can order me around after you're officially crowned." He grinned, lifting my other glove so he could slide it over my hand. Niklaus brushed his fingers along the inside of my forearm and raised a brow.

If I thought he'd listen to my orders, perhaps I would. Niklaus stood before me dressed in fine clothing, with his hair combed to the side. I missed his wayward locks, but for the ceremony, I could tolerate his polished appearance and mess his hair later on.

"Truly, if I thought it were possible . . ." My words trailed off, and he lifted a finger to his lips.

Niklaus flourished a bow, extending his hand. "My soon-to-be queen, the carriage awaits, and I'd rather not be blamed for you being late to your own coronation."

I narrowed my eyes, slapping my gloved hand into his. "We all know it'd be your fault, anyway."

He tugged me against his chest, smirking. Dipping his head down, he kissed the tip of my nose and released me.

"Don't tempt me."

The ride to the cathedral wasn't as I expected, although to be honest, I wasn't sure what to expect. My father had been king when I was born, and I'd never witnessed a coronation myself. However, with Lord Aksel's aid, we were able to appoint a new bishop to help.

The streets were lined with hundreds of individuals. They threw bouquets and petals onto the road as the carriage traveled along.

When we reached the cathedral, Alric moved beside me and escorted us inside the building. The pews were filled with dignitaries, mostly those that held a position in our newly formed Council, but also those of foreign blood. Abendrot's new alliances and those of old. The Seidels were there, and Raif and Frederik too.

A blond head stood out from the rest. It turned, and Ashroy's profile held a smirk. He inclined his head as we passed him and made it to the pulpit.

Niklaus pulled away, making his way down toward Ashroy. The bishop handed me a scepter. It felt heavy in my grasp, but the ceremony began, whether or not I was ready.

I repeated the ceremonial words when prompted, speaking them with everything that I was. It was only when the bishop placed the heavy crown on my head, announcing that I was Abendrot's queen, that I realized it was over.

The congregation stood, applauding, but my eyes found Niklaus, then Ashroy, who stood next to Edda.

The road to this moment hadn't been paved in gold, and my heart was heavy with that notion. But it was every act, every misstep, and every unfortunate event that had brought me here and closer to those I loved, and those I found along the way.

It was time for Abendrot's healing, and mine too.

Epilogue

A nervous buzz hung in the air, churning my stomach and tightening my chest. I couldn't believe this was happening. It had been almost two years since the coronation, and Niklaus, to my surprise, suggested we wait to marry until things had settled.

His words were: "Let the kingdom settle and recover. I'm not going anywhere—you made certain of that."

So, we waited. Every inch of the way, he was there by my side, allowing me to sound off, stumble, and sometimes even fall. Each time he'd lift me, smirk, and suggest I try something else.

Captain Alric was slow to forgive Niklaus' transgressions, but he did. Alric watched him carefully in every meeting, every gathering, and when Niklaus would venture home, Alric expressed his distrust. Eventually, everyone relaxed into the new normal—except Alric, who maintained his strong dislike for Niklaus and only tolerated him for my sake.

"It isn't too late to change your mind, you know. You could leave him standing at the altar and no one would question it." Alric stood with his arms folded across his chest, his dark brows furrowing.

I laughed but felt my stomach lurch from the nerves. My throat felt as though it were about to close. This was just another ceremony for the public because there was no decree from the bishop that was stronger than what we shared.

"You know I won't. Besides, he has proven himself, and you can't deny that."

"Unfortunately." He smiled wryly. In a moment, the smile turned genuine as he took in my appearance. "You look beautiful."

Since my father's passing, Alric had been more of a father than my own had been. When I needed him, he was there. He trusted and valued my voice and for that, I'd always be grateful.

"Thank you."

I chanced a glimpse at myself in the full-length mirror. My silver-spun hair coiled on the top of my head, with curled strands by my cheeks. The gown I wore was ivory in color, with accents of gold. I looked very much like one of the old paintings in the castle: poised, with an unreadable expression and not as terrified as I felt.

Alric pushed off the wall and toward me. "It's a ceremony, that's all. You're only confirming what is already known to the court, remember that."

He didn't move forward to embrace me, that would be far too personal, and Alric tried his best to keep me at a distance. He had said I was like the daughter he never had more than once.

His words didn't soothe my nerves, though. I sighed, trying not to rub my kohl-lined eyes. "I know." To my surprise, I felt arms around me.

"You are the Wolf Queen," Alric said as he withdrew. His fingers caught my chin, and he winked. "Fear isn't a lack of courage, Stasya. Fear is normal. Courage is carrying on even though you're terrified. You, my dear, are one of the most courageous individuals I know."

Tears pooled in my eyes, but I refused to let them fall. I'd not smudge my eyes before I made it to the cathedral. "Thank you, Alric, truly." I cleared my throat, also clearing my head. "I'm ready now."

Outside, Alric escorted me into the carriage, and then we were off. I was taken aback to see the crowds along the roads. The people waved to the carriage, tossed bouquets and oats to the ground in celebration. I couldn't greet them yet, not until after the ceremony.

It was a long, torturous half hour before we arrived at the cathedral. Music blared from inside the stone structure, and if I'd thought the roadsides had many people, there were even more here.

"I can still sneak you out of here," Alric offered teasingly.

"Oh, stop." I laughed and steadied myself. "I'm ready."

Alric opened the door, and the crowd grew silent, as if they were holding their breaths. All of that for me? I stepped down from the carriage, someone handed me a bouquet, and then I walked for what seemed like miles, until I was inside the building and staring at Niklaus.

He wore a dark green doublet with a golden sash crossing his body, and breeches tucked into knee-high boots. Gloves covered his hands, and a sword hung from his hip. Groomed like this, he didn't look like a butcher's son or an assassin. Instead, he looked the part of a royal. His hair was even slicked back and off to the side instead of jutting upward in wayward spikes.

I heard nothing save for the thrumming of my heart and Niklaus, and it was only when I was prompted that I recited the vows.

"I now pronounce you united beneath the moon and sun. Let no one come between you. You may kiss your bride," the bishop announced.

I don't think anyone was prepared for the kiss Niklaus had in store for me. I know that I wasn't, not in front of everyone like this. He moved forward, closing the distance between us, and pressed his lips against mine. It started off chaste enough, and then his mouth opened so his tongue could dance against mine. I knew what he was doing. It was an open display that I was his, but it went both ways, for he was also mine.

The bishop cleared his throat, and when we turned to face the inhabitants of the cathedral, a collective cheer rang out. It was done. We were wed.

LONG AFTER THE wedding celebrations had ended, Elka helped pry the pins from my hair. "Tonight will be the first night you are husband and wife. I have something that will make it special." She clucked her tongue and ducked around the privacy screen to pull something out. "It's from east of Ishkertov. One of my cousins had been traveling through . . . It's made of worm silk! Imagine that." Elka slid it over my figure and bit her lip. "Nik will be beside himself." She laughed. "Do you need anything else?"

"No, that'll be all." I grinned. This wouldn't be the first time Niklaus and I had been together, but it would be different, or at least, I imagined it would.

A knock on the suite's door interrupted my thoughts, and I raced to it. "Yes?"

"Let me in," Niklaus drawled.

"Or what?" I teased.

"I'll huff, I'll puff, and I'll kick this bloody door in. Don't deny your husband."

My husband, I thought, shivering in excitement. "As your queen, you will refrain from speaking to me in such a manner." I opened the door a crack, eyeing him. Niklaus was still dressed in his formal attire, which made me want to peel it off of him layer by layer. "I expect you to grovel."

He pushed the door open the rest of the way and threw me over his shoulder, eliciting a surprised *yip.*

"I beg for my queen's mercy," he drawled, his voice laced with sarcasm as he flipped me onto the bed.

I landed on my back, cheeks flushed as I stared up at him. "I'll pardon you, this once. Only because I hate to see the Big Bad Wolf begging."

He grunted in disapproval but said nothing. Niklaus' eyes roamed my body. "What is this?" He mused out loud, touching the strap with his roughened fingers. He watched as the fabric easily slid along my skin, and he grinned.

"It's silk. Do you like it?" His touch awakened every nerve ending in my body.

"I do. But what is this about the Big Bad Wolf begging?" He leaned forward, lips brushing against mine.

"I ordered you to beg. I am a merciful queen." I hissed as his teeth nipped along my neck.

"You are, indeed. Long live the queen."

I silenced him with my lips. I would savor this moment for the rest of our lifetime, the first time together as more than mates. We were wolves, and we were equally matched.

Long live the reign of wolves.

Acknowledgments

First and foremost, I want to thank **you** the reader, for making your way to the end of this series. It's hard to believe that this is the end of Niklaus and Stasya's story. When I published Hunter's Truce in October of 2018, I never imagined it would take off as it has. For that, I'm extremely grateful to all of you who've made it a success.

Even though this is the last Nik and Stasya story, I hope you continue following me on writing journey

To my editor, Meg Dailey, thank you, thank you, thank you for polishing my baby up! You are a godsend, honestly! Storytelling may be my forte, but grammar is NOT.

Yentl, I wrote that epilogue just for you, sweets! I am so grateful to have you in my life. I cherish our friendship more than you could ever know. I love you.

Christis Christie and Lou Wilham, my original Writing Squad—what can I say except thank you? You guys are seriously my rock. You're there as my sounding board, as my rocks, as my cheerleaders, and so much more. To say that I love you simply doesn't cut it, but it'll have to do.

A huge thank you to my *MiTiWriMo* girls, without our torturous sprints, these new scenes wouldn't exist.

Massive kisses and thank you's to my entire family for enduring my writing sprees, which is writer-speak for clocking out mentally to escape into our made up world. I love you guys so much!

You all can thank Danielle M. for the inspiration behind the bonus scene. She won a giveaway, which was her choice of a scene! She desperately wanted to see Heidi–Niklaus' mother–in her element before King Ansgar ruled and ruined everything. So, huge shout out to Danielle!

Also, in case you forgot–Gregor is Nik's father, and I thought it'd be fun to show Heidi meeting him for the first time. He was never a good guy, and wasn't ever supposed to be. Gregor was King Aslaug's attack dog, and he never went anywhere without him. He knew that Gregor was a were- wolf, and used that to his advantage. This was also where Ansgar's hatred for werewolves started, too. Not just because Stasya was later turned, but Ansgar's father almost favored Gregor more than his own flesh and blood!

Anyway, I hope you guys enjoyed this bonus! Again, thank you Danielle. Without you, this scene would never exist. I hope you all enjoyed it.

The Official Playlist

Want to listen along while you read and immerse yourself into the world of The Hunter? Listen to the playlist below!

1. Drown Me In Your Love by Jacquie
2. I Won't Back Down by Swon Brothers
3. Alive by Sia
4. Devil Side by Foxes
5. Here With Me by Susie Suh
6. Castle by Halsey
7. What I Did For Love by Emeli Sandé
8. Torpedo by Jillette Johnson
9. Healing by Tim Chaisson
10. Walking My Way by Tyler Brown Williams

About Elle Beaumont

Elle Beaumont loves creating vivid and fantastical worlds. She lives in Southeastern Massachusetts with her husband and two children. When not writing or chasing around her children, she enjoys making candles. More than once she has proclaimed that coffee is the lifeblood and it is how she refrains from becoming a zombie.

Stay up to date and receive some free books by signing up for her newsletter! ellebeaumontbooks.com/newsletter

Join Elle's Facebook group and hang out with her facebook.com/groups/ElleBeaumontStreetTeam

For more information visit
www.ellebeaumontbooks.com
Follow Elle on social media!

facebook.com/ellebeaumontbooks
instagram.com/ellebeaumontbooks

MORE FROM ELLE
* TITLES AVAILABLE IN KINDLE UNLIMITED

Standalones

The Castle of Thorns

The Dragon's Bride*

Beneath the Willow

Benvolio & Mercutio Turn Back Time

Immortal Realms Trilogy

Seeds of Sorrow

Tides of Torment

Wages of War

The Hunter Series

Hunter's Truce*

Royal's Vow*

Assassin's Gambit*

Queen's Edge*

Secrets of Galathea

Brotherhood

Bindings

Voice

King

Of Flames & Curses by Whitney L. Spradling

Do fairies exist?

This is the question Lainey asks herself after her sister's brutal murder in Central Park. Armed with her sister's diary and the mysterious entries within, Lainey's quest for answers leads her to Phoenix, a surly but handsome fae.

The answer to Lainey's question reveals a truth that will change everything she thought she knew about herself and the world she lives in. A sacrifice must be made to break a curse that locked the gate between the human and faerie realms.

Leaving the only world she has known, Lainey finds herself surrounded by evil queens, curses, and magical creatures. Together, Lainey and Phoenix must find a way to break the curse that doesn't result in Lainey's death—like her sister's.

Available Now

Bound Island by G.D. Roman

Brye, Lenna, and Tara have lived their entire lives on an island surrounded by mists and protected by magical bonds. Nothing could be more perfect. Until one night, when magic begins to fray at the seams, and their lives change forever.

The Healer – Brye's healing abilities are her pride, making her the best match of the season. If only someone were interesting enough for her. Until she catches the eye of Prince Gareth, the least interesting one of all.

The Mist Maiden – Lenna has lived her life in the shadow of her sisters. Until Beltane, when her magic explodes. Now, she has been chosen to be a Mist Maiden, protector of Avalon. A role she was never destined to play.

The Warrior – Tara knows that she is meant to be more than being someone's mate. A warrior through and through, Tara strives for the extraordinary. No matter the cost. Even if that means she might have to sacrifice her growing feelings for Aiden.

As Avalon slowly becomes an island lost in the mists, will the sisters strengthen their bonds and save their home, or will they break apart forever?

Available Now

The Songs That Beckon by M.A. Brown

Their grief binds them
The Song calls them
The Darkness wants to claim them

As winter wraps Areth in its frozen embrace, nightmarish beasts descend upon the Hastings household kidnapping Mr. and Mrs. Hastings and leaving behind their daughter, Bianca, as sole witness. In the wake of their abduction her quiet world is turned upside down and shaken revealing the secrets and lies her parents have buried.

As truths unravel it binds her to those who have similarly lost. Together they must wade through the thorny tangles of growing love and grief to find those that they hold dear before the looming threat of darkness is unleashed to destroy them all.

Available Now